LOOSE ENDS

John Walling

Published by Riparian Publishing
5 Tonnant Way
Great Grimsby
North East Lincolnshire

ISBN 978-0-9523848-4-7

British Library Cataloguing in Publication Data
A catalogue record for this book is available from the British Library

This story is fiction.

Printed and bound in the UK by CPI Antony Rowe Limited
Bumper's Farm Industrial Estate, Chippenham. Wiltshire

CONTENTS

LOOSE ENDS

PART ONE

CHAPTER ONE

But for the war Detective Chief Inspector Alistair McIntosh would have retired from the force in 1940. By that time he would have served his required thirty years to enable him to live a comfortable life on a well-earned pension, but he was persuaded to remain in the Glasgow Central Division until 'the end of hostilities' as his superintendent had put it. If the war was going to go on for a long time it was anticipated that a shortage of new recruits would develop and, together with the inevitability of increased duties, it would put a great strain on the police resources. So, along with others who had served their time, he was asked to stay - although he knew that he could not really refuse as the request had come from a very high authority.

In the spring of 1945, the Allied Forces were closing in on the remains of the German Army and all but the Third Reich were confident that the Allies would soon be victorious. By the middle of April there was very little of Western Germany that was unoccupied, along with the Eastern part of the country, with Russian troops moving fast towards Berlin.

Chief Inspector McIntosh was looking forward to a quieter life, and had promised himself that he would retire as soon as the last shot had been fired. He scanned the newspapers eagerly, almost ticking off the days to his well-earned rest. He hoped that the only major case left to deal with could be given to the U.S. Army authorities in this country to solve.

The body of an American soldier had emerged from the depths of the Clyde about twelve miles from Glasgow half a mile down river from the bridge at Bothwell. It seemed of little consequence

to Alistair and he thought that it was probably the result of yet another case of trouble in the inevitable conflict between black and white Americans. However, he was given the task of looking into the circumstances of the death, thankfully knowing that if the soldier had been stabbed there would be very little chance of finding out who had done it. Alistair took his time driving the black police saloon to the hospital mortuary where the body had been taken.
Running his hand over the top of his almost bald head he hesitated before entering the room that he had visited so many times. He hoped this would be the last time. Fastening the two buttons of his well-worn double-breasted suit jacket and, covering most of his face with his handkerchief, he strode authoritatively towards where the severely emaciated naked body lay on the table.
He had seen many dead bodies laid out like this but each one was different. He had become quite blasé about looking at corpses feeling neither emotion nor concern about what lay there. There had been a few exceptions, especially when a young girl had been murdered. He had no children of his own but looking at the face of a teenage girl, her young body covered in stab wounds, or her neck broken by some sadistic monster, he found almost unbearable. However, he had no such inhibitions looking at the dead bodies of adults. Maybe it was because he had seen so many!
To Alistair there were no immediately obvious signs of how this man had died and whether he had been murdered or just drowned.
"Have you discovered the cause of death?"
"I don't think there is any doubt about it, Alistair," said the police pathologist, looking over the top of his rimless spectacles. "I can certainly tell you that he didn’t fall in, nor did he drown. I believe that he died of asphyxiation due to constriction of the neck by the fact that the hyoid bone had been fractured which could be consistent with manual strangulation.
"You mean someone grabbed him there and squeezed hard with their hands?"
"Well, most probably as far as I can tell from this bloated body, but if it helps, it would certainly have to be a strong man who did

that in my opinion. But you're the detective, Alistair, it's my job to tell you how he died. It's your job to find out who that somebody was, but there's no doubt that he was dead before he was put into the water. And by the way, there are still a few marks round the ankles which suggests that he had something tied to them, probably to keep him down, which obviously came loose."
"How long has he been in there?"
"Difficult to tell accurately now because of the state of the body, but I should think something under a couple of weeks."
"Couple of weeks!" The inspector had been hoping, before he came, that if it had happened during the last couple of days he might have been able to clear the thing up quite quickly, but two weeks! Not much hope of that now.
"Well, as I said, not very easy to be certain of the time when a body has been in a mucky river, but more accurately perhaps, could only be ten days or so."
"Is that all you can tell me?"
"Well, he's male, but then you can probably see that; could be about twenty-plus years of age and by his uniform, an American G.I., but then you knew all that before you came." He was grinning at the inspector.
"Okay, stop dragging it out. What else have we got to go on?" Alistair thought that he had not been told everything and was beginning to lose his patience. He just wanted to go home and leave all this to the U.S. Army to deal with.
The pathologist looked at the inspector and put his hand into the pocket of his white coat "Oh yes, I almost forgot," he teased, and held out his hand to the inspector. "This identity tag was still around his neck."

Two days later an American Lieutenant telephoned. The body was that of a Private Joseph Peabody, reported as a deserter from the 1st American Army sometime in February. The Lieutenant would appreciate the cooperation from the Glasgow police in trying to find the killer and enclosed a number of photographs.

Detective Chief Inspector Alistair McIntosh's heart sank. This was just what he could have done without during his last days in the force. He had visions of his retirement being delayed even further. He decided to try the newspapers first and gave the photos that had been sent to him as well as the story, to both the local press and the national papers, asking them to make a bit of a headline of it. He also requested them to make an appeal for anyone who knew the American or who might have seen him. After all, many girls became very friendly with American soldiers and there would no doubt be someone who would have remembered him. The "Daily Mirror" made a bit of a splash about the story in half a column of the centre pages a few days later.

CHAPTER TWO

Cornelius Hill, the landlord of the "Cricketer's Arms" in the village of Western, in Dorset was an avid reader of the "Daily Mirror." He had kept the inn since the early 1930s and now aged 50 he had always tried to create the image of 'a friendly mine host.' But it wasn't always that easy. In December 1939 his wife had died of a sudden heart attack followed by the loss of his only son six months later, killed on the beaches of Dunkirk. During that terrible first year of the war, he managed to keep going with the support of some of his loyal customers and their wives, who helped him in every way they could.

The following year a young lady from the village came to ask for a job. She had recently come to live with her aunt after the loss of her parents in an early bombing raid in London. Because of what he had suffered, Cornelius immediately felt sorry for the girl, knowing what she must have been going through, and employed her straight away. After all, he thought that it wouldn't do his trade any harm to have a good-looking young barmaid to help cheer up the place, and it developed into a kind of father and daughter relationship.

With the shortage of beer and most of the local men in the forces, the last four years had been a struggle, but now with the end of the war imminent, he was much more relaxed and was leaning over the bar casually glancing through his favourite newspaper. After first finding out what Jane was up to in the popular cartoon strip on the back page, and, to see whether she had removed her dress yet again, he turned to the middle pages and saw the headline, "American Soldier Strangled."

The story told of how a Joseph Peabody, a G.I. had been strangled and had been discovered in the river Clyde on the outskirts of Glasgow. The news item said that the police were asking the public for their help and if any one recognised his picture, or his name, to contact them immediately.

"Hey, Liz," he called to his attractive barmaid, "Come and look at this, here's a picture of Joe, your old boyfriend. You never did tell me the full story of why you were going to Scotland with him."
The colour drained from Elizabeth's face as she looked at the picture. Dead? She couldn't believe it. How could he be dead and what could have possibly happened to him?
"I told you before that I wasn't exactly going to Scotland *with* him. I was going, to see my aunt in Glasgow as I said before, we just travelled together, that's all" She could not possibly tell him the real reason why she and Joe had been going to Scotland or what had happened afterwards. She had to think quickly.
Cornelius had noticed how unhappy she had been since her return but every time he had asked what was wrong she just shrugged her shoulders and said, "Oh! nothing really." He was aware of her relationship with Joe and assumed she was unhappy because he had obviously jilted her.
She looked again at the photograph and Cornelius could see how upset she appeared. "Murdered?" she said out loud. "How? Why?" Whatever had happened during her stay in Glasgow she felt distraught at learning that he was dead and, more especially, of how he had died.
Her employer noticed the tears in her eyes and put his hand over hers in a gesture of condolence.
"What an end for poor old Joe", he said sadly. "I suppose I'd better let the police know that he used to come here. This report says that the police are asking if anyone knew him and of course we did. If we don't tell them and they find out that we are withholding information, we'd be in serious trouble."
At that moment, everything that had happened flashed through Elizabeth's mind in an instant. She began to panic. She had to try to persuade him not to say anything to anyone about Joe's visits.
"We can't do that....you see..." she hesitated for a moment, wondering if it was the right for him to know the truth, "...you see, Neil...he wasn't on leave when he came here...he was a deserter and on the run. The police wouldn't believe that we didn't know,

and, we'd be in worse trouble if they found out he'd been hiding here!"
The landlord knew that when she called him Neil, she was either up to something or was asking for his support. He looked aghast, let go of her hand and opened his mouth to speak, but Elizabeth kept talking.
"And what about me? I wasn't involved with his death and I don't know who was, but do you think the police would believe that I had nothing to do with it if they found out that we had left here together to go to Scotland? You didn't tell anyone else that we'd set off together on the same train did you?" She pleaded to her employer her hands tightly clasped.
The landlord shook his head. "I told the customers that you'd gone to Scotland to see your aunt - as you said. When he didn't come back everyone assumed that Joe had returned to his unit, but you never told me that he was a deserter." He wagged his finger at her in a threatening manner. "You've now put me in a very difficult position. Liz."
"So you see, please, don't say anything to the police about either of us will you? To tell them that I was with him won’t help them find out who killed him. It would only get us both involved."
Cornelius bowed his head looking down to the floor contemplating what she had said and trying to make sense of it all. "Well, it looks now that you've given me no option. Let's hope that none of my customers recognise him from the paper. If they do, I'll have to tell them that we've already reported it," he concluded, somewhat reluctantly. "Unless of course someone noticed you together on the train," he added as an afterthought, looking directly at her.
She avoided his gaze and turned to walk away hoping that she had convinced him to keep quiet.
Cornelius watched her leave as he gave the matter some further thought before deciding that she was probably right and, perhaps under the circumstances, it would be better if he said nothing. Trying to forget it, he turned back to the front page of the Mirror to read about how the Allies were closing in on Berlin, and to the

war correspondent's report that the war in Europe would soon be over.
Elizabeth went to her room to go over all that had happened since she had last seen Joe, but she still couldn't take it all in that he had been murdered. What she had never told her employer, was at Carlisle station, Joe had got off the Glasgow train for a few seconds to meet someone, and was certain that she'd seen him arrested on the platform.
On her return journey to Dorset following her stay in Glasgow, she too had left the train at Carlisle and wondered if she could find out what had happened to Joe. She thought that the railway porter might know or perhaps where the American M.Ps had taken him. But instead she had been taken to the police station there and she had been questioned. She had pretended not to know Joe except for him being a travelling companion and was asking purely out of curiosity But now, because Joe had been murdered, she thought that they would tell the police in charge of the investigation in Glasgow about her asking about him and they would probably conclude that she had known more about the American soldier than she had told them at the time.
"Oh my God! Now what shall I do?" she said out loud.
She also began to worry about her sailor friend, Howard. She had told the Carlisle police when she was interviewed, that the three of them had travelled together in the same carriage and they had asked her where Howard was stationed. After the American had left, she assumed that she would never see Joe again and took up a relationship with the sailor, which inevitably developed into an intimate relationship for a few days in Glasgow. She had even fallen in love with him and he with her and they dreamed of having a wonderful future together but then everything went wrong.

It wasn't Howard's fault when things didn't work out as planned and she returned to London without even saying goodbye.

Since her return he had not been out of her mind and although she had often thought of writing to him to apologise for going as she did, she never got round to it.
But now the situation had changed and she knew that she must see him again, especially because of what he might tell the police if they went to interview him at Paisley where he was stationed.She began to feel very frightened and lay down on the bed, her body shaking.
The last time she had felt as scared as this was four years ago in London. She recalled that time and everything that had happened to her since.

CHAPTER THREE

Elizabeth Harrison had been born in a terraced house in Earl Street close to Liverpool Street Station. Her parents had been killed in the first daylight raid on London during the second year of the war. She had been working as a trainee ladies hairdresser in a shop in the city at the time when the air raid siren had sounded, and had spent the next few hours, along with hundreds of others, in the Leicester Square Underground station sheltering from the bombing. She would never forget that day, and the feeling of horror when she finally managed to reach home to find the houses in Earl Street reduced to rubble. There was no sign of the house where she had been born and she was met by the Street Warden who gave her the sad news that both her parents were dead.
Her father had spent all his life working at Smithfield Market from leaving school at aged fourteen and her mother had had a hard time looking after the home and bringing up their three children. She had adored them both and was grief stricken.. Elizabeth's two brothers were older than her and both had been killed within a few weeks of each other in 1940. Arthur lost his life during the Allied armies' retreat to Dunkirk and Donald, who was in the Navy, died when his ship exploded just off the coast whilst taking the men off the beaches during the evacuation.
Now at only sixteen she was left all alone and, along with others she knew who had also lost families, tried to put on a brave face convincing herself that she must quickly get on with her life as best she could. After the funerals, she left London and went to live with her aunt in a village in Dorset where she found a job as a barmaid in the local pub, the "Cricketer's Arms."
She was a pretty girl with a good figure. Her long straight well groomed auburn hair, which almost reached her shoulders, ended in a neat roll at the bottom. She had an infectious smile and soon the customers loved her. The trouble was that one or two of the soldiers took advantage of her and she became involved with them The landlord turned a blind eye to her 'goings on', as he called it, and, as long as it did not interfere with her work, he did not

complain. After all, having an attractive barmaid did bring business into his pub, but feeling a certain amount of responsibility he did warn her on more than one occasion to be careful. However, local gossip soon put an end to the good relationship that she and her aunt had enjoyed, and she told Elizabeth to leave her house and find accommodation elsewhere. Fortunately, the landlord had a small cottage, which he said she could rent while she remained in the job.

Life in the village went on happily and the pub became busier with increasing numbers of British soldiers moving into the area after a while. Then later, American soldiers who had arrived in England, also began visiting the village public houses on a regular basis. Liz became very friendly with a tall handsome G.I. called Joe. He brought her things that young girls at that time found it almost impossible to obtain, showering her with gifts of nylons, perfume, and chocolates and making her feel very special. For the first time since her parents had died she had met someone who appeared to respect and love her, and her relationship with Joe made her realise that she was wasting her life. He repeatedly told her that he loved her and Elizabeth was enchanted with him. She had never previously experienced the wonderful exciting feelings she had when they made love and wanted to be with him all the time. However, he only managed to see her at irregular intervals, each one seeming an eternity to Liz.

When together they chatted easily to each other, Liz opening her heart to him about the life she had been living since her parents had been killed. Joe was very understanding about what she had been through, and made light of what had been her unfortunate way of life before they had met.

He told her about his ranch in Texas and how he would take her to his home in America when the war was over. "You'll love it there Honey and we'll get married and have lots of kids" - and she, in her naivety, believed every word he said. But after a while a feeling of mistrust began to sour their relationship.

He boasted to her how he had acquired the things he had brought, most of which he admitted were stolen. When she admonished him over it, he remarked, "But that's what happens in war, Honey. Lots of things just get left lying about belonging to nobody, see?" She couldn't bring herself to condone the things that he had done until, finally, she begged him not to bring any more gifts unless he got them honestly.
During the spring of 1944 his visits to the inn stopped, and rumours spread that the invasion of France was imminent.

CHAPTER FOUR

Marine Commando Andy McKern had been specially trained to serve with the 1st Special Service Brigade, under the command of Lord Lovat, and had landed with his comrades on Sword Beach on D.Day. During the following eight months as the Allies advanced through France and Belgium, the fighting had been intense. His unit was usually in the forefront of most of the attacks and he had considered himself to be extremely fortunate not to have been wounded from either shrapnel or bullet during this time. However, during a brief reconnoitre with two other marines in order to try and ascertain the enemy's position, he had been hit by a German sniper's bullet and was now aboard a small ship returning to England.

The bullet had damaged the bone in his left shoulder, affecting the nerves, causing numbness in his arm right down to the end of his fingers. The limb was practically useless and he kept it close to his body in a large sling until he would be able to get it seen to by a surgeon at Glasgow Royal Infirmary. Andy knew that his war was most certainly over, and he was looking forward to being able to get back to Scotland as soon as possible, leave the Army and then hope to return to his old job in the city.

Andy had been an assistant to a reputable jeweller who had a shop in the centre of Glasgow but always ready to make a little on the side, he was friendly with a so-called diamond merchant who rented small premises in a back-alley off Sauchiehall Street. Charlie MacKenzie's small shop was well known. It was the place where young couples of limited means could purchase diamond engagement rings for a very low price - at least, they looked like real diamonds but were really just costume jewellery. However, Charlie MacKenzie did not deceive any of his customers. He always told them exactly what they were purchasing, but if there was a shady deal to be done in diamonds in Glasgow, both Andy and Charlie MacKenzie were almost certain to be involved.

Why Andy had volunteered to join a specialist section of commandos was something he had often wondered about. He was

only five feet and a few inches tall and a stocky little man with a fine pair of strong legs. He had often told the story that his lack of height gave him an advantage in the fighting, as he considered that most of the bullets fired in his direction would go over his head. However, until this last one found its target, the risks he had taken had been exciting and challenging, and he had experienced feelings not unlike those he had had when he had been involved in those illicit deals with Charlie MacKenzie before the war, but the danger then was of being arrested, not shot!
Many of the friends he had made while serving in the army had been killed, and he considered himself to be very lucky not to have been wounded before this last encounter. Although he had felt anger at the time and used some very strong language about the German who had shot him, he was pleased that he was still alive and finished with the fighting.

After leaving the harbour at Calais, he was only a couple miles out on an old small cruise liner which was being used as a hospital ship leaning over the rails wondering why he'd bothered to have such a big breakfast! He had never been a good sailor. When they had all gone over the English Channel on D.Day during that long and horrendous sea voyage to Normandy, he had been seasick for a good part of the way. On that day, with heavy seas and a strong wind, many of the men had also suffered in the same way, although then it had not only been the pitch and toss of the boat which had caused the nausea, but the fear of what lay ahead on those fortified beaches, and whether they would still be alive at the end of that first, and what proved to be, a terribly long day.
Due to the Allies' supremacy both in the air and on the sea during these last few months of the war, there was no need for that sort of anxiety for their safety on this particular journey as they crossed the English Channel, but it was now only the movement of the ship which caused him to feel ill. He pulled his coat around him with his one good arm, trying to keep himself warm. As he did so, he was aware of another unfortunate victim only a few yards along the rail, suffering in the same way as himself. He recognised

the olive-green and well-tailored but badly soiled uniform of an American G.I., wearing a Red-Cross armband. The American soldier moved along the rail towards him and put his hand on Andy's good shoulder.
"How yer doin' fella? I'm Joe," he said in a tired and weak voice. His face looked drawn and bloodless. He too was shivering.
Andy mumbled his own name and, noticing the American's pale complexion, remarked, "Och! You look as fuckin' bad as I feel."
They stood for a while watching the white crests of the black waves dancing in the moonlight, until the American, throwing away what was left of his cigarette, said that he was feeling a little better and suggested that they ought to go back inside the ship into the warmth.
"I think I'd rather die of sea-sickness inside the ship than get bloody freezin' cold out here. What d'yer say, Andy?"
The Scotsman agreed. "Aye, I suppose it's worth risking."
Once inside, they sat quietly smoking their cigarettes for a while, trying to get the circulation working back into their cold bodies before either of them felt like any conversation. The American was the first to speak.
"Did yer come over on D. Day, an' what'yer done to yourself, Andy?" Joe pointed to the Scotsman's sling and heavily bandaged shoulder, "or was it a fuckin' son-of-a-bitch German gave it to yer?" he asked.
Andy had no intention of giving this fellow his life history, but explained briefly his time spent in the army as modestly as possible, then pointing to his bandaged shoulder, "Bin' through four years of this fuckin' war and then some Jerry bastard gi'me this."
He was not particularly over the moon with fondness for Americans and was careful not to give away any secrets in case the fellow turned out to be somebody different from what he appeared. However, he thought that if he struck up a conversation with him it might help to take his mind off the unpleasant journey and the fact that he was on board a ship with thousands of feet of

water underneath him. It might also help to forget the pain he was suffering.
They talked about their lives before the war and Andy could see no harm in telling him about his civilian life in Glasgow and his time in the jewellery trade before he went into the army.
It reminded him of how much he wanted to get back and forget all about the war. He was also aware of the reputation of some G.Is to 'shoot-a-line', so he thought that there would be no harm in boasting that he knew enough about diamonds to be almost an expert. "I'll be able t'get a job quite easy in the trade when I get oot o' the army, so, Joe, if you want any cheap diamonds to take back to America, I'm your man," he joked.
Joe listened intently to what his new-found acquaintance was saying, especially when he talked about his knowledge of diamonds. It was a lucky coincidence that he had met someone who knew something about them, as Joe had a bag full inside his tunic pocket. Could he trust him? Would he know their value if he showed them to him? But would he then want to know how they had been acquired?
Andy had joked about getting involved with some shady deals in the jewellery trade, even boasted about it. Surely he could trust him if he offered him a good deal. Joe had wondered previously how he could get rid of the diamonds and now luck had brought this devious character to him who could probably help him to turn them into money.
"Could yer put a value on some diamonds by just looking at 'em?" Joe asked.
"Well, nae really," Andy explained. "Diamonds are a very complicated business, and valuing 'em depends on many things."
"Couldn't yer even gi'me a very rough estimate of, say, a handful?" the American asked.
"I could tell if they were fuckin' genuine or no', but the value wi' depend on lots of things including the size of each stone and a number of other things which determines the price. Why d'you want to know?" If this fellow had a few diamonds he would be interested, and maybe could do well for himself at the same time.

Joe hesitated as he considered whether or not to give out more information. He was somewhat reluctant to tell this Scotsman, who he had only just met, any details about where he had obtained the diamonds. He wondered whether it would be safe to do so, but really he had no option other than to tell him something if he wanted to get rid of them.. Perhaps if he told Andy enough to satisfy him he would not be questioned further.

CHAPTER FIVE

The American looked closely into the Scotsman's face before answering his question. Surely, he said to himself, he would be foolish to miss this opportunity of doing a deal with someone who knew about diamonds. He decided that he would tell him only so much to see how it went. He could easily make up a story.
"Somebody gave me some and then gotten themselves killed," Joe explained. It was partly true, but he wasn't going tell a stranger what had really happened. "If yer know somebody in your world who could give me a good price for them or if you could sell ‘em for me, well that would be swell. How about it, buddy?"
"Where are they? Can I see 'em?" Andy tried to sound very calm because he knew that if he had reacted in any other way Joe might lose his confidence in being able to trust him. He had dealt with situations like this before.
"I've got the packet inside my tunic. My bag is over there with the rest of my things," Joe said, pointing to a slightly better lit area, "so maybe we could er...use that corner?"
Andy corrected him. "It's nae a packet, it's what we call in the trade, a parcel of diamonds, but whatever you want to call 'em there's nae enough fuckin’ light there either to enable me to examine them carefully enough. Could we find somewhere d'y're think wi' even a better light?"
Joe rummaged around in his bag and produced a large metal torch. It clinked against a bottle, and Joe just winked and whispered, "A bottle o' champagne. Keep it quiet. Okay?"
Andy wondered what else he might be carrying. Diamonds and champagne were enoug h to cause him to suspect that this fellow was not telling him the truth about how he had acquired these things. If he asked, he expected that this American would tell him that someone gave him the champagne as well!
Joe looked around to ensure that no one else could see what they were doing before taking the bag out from the inside pocket of his tunic. He spread the diamonds out over his handkerchief and switched on the torch.

"If you shine the torch over them for me I can maybe gi' thee some idea." Andy couldn't believe his eyes. "Fuckin' hell, mon! Who the fuck gave you this lot?"
There were far more than he had expected to see, estimating that there must have been a few dozen or more stones: all of different sizes: some even quite large. He knew immediately that these hadn't been given to this American, but thought it best to say nothing at this stage.

"I'd really need an eyeglass to examine them properly," Andy explained under his breath. "I'm nae an expert, but there must be fuckin' thousands and thousands of pounds worth here!" Without taking his eyes off the diamonds under the torchlight, he added, "If we could weigh 'em to determine the amount of carats, then I could perhaps gie a price nearer to their value, subject, of course, to a proper examination." Andy was aware that he would be nowhere near the real value as each one would have to be examined carefully to ascertain their true worth, but he quickly saw that he could be on to a good thing, as the Yank obviously knew absolutely nothing about the value of the stones he had.
"Where did your friend get 'em?" Andy asked innocently, still looking closely at each stone. He would be intrigued to hear Joe's answer but at the same time was determined to handle the situation very carefully.
Joe had anticipated the question and was ready with his answer. A minimum of truth would be all that was necessary. "Some town in Belgium, I think he'd said."
Andy was now more convinced than ever that he was not being told the truth. If he had said Amsterdam he would have been more impressed but he knew that would have been impossible as there was little or no Allied occupation or fighting in Holland.
Joe was astonished at Andy's first estimate of their worth - thousands and thousands of pounds he had said. He decided to act quickly. "If yer can get that sort of price for 'em, ten per cent's yours."
Andy nodded his head, partly in agreement of the ten per cent, and partly because he was confident that he knew where he could find

a buyer. "They should have some accurate scales in the dispensary on board for weighing ounces, so let's go and see."
They found what they were looking for, and Andy was not surprised to discover that the diamonds weighed more than he thought. He said nothing until they went back to the quiet corner they had left, and then he began to try to calculate a figure that he thought would satisfy the American. Even by just looking at them he knew that, being genuine, they would be worth a great deal of money.
"Jewels are usually valued by how many carats of each one," Andy began, and not wanting to sound too excited while trying to recall the way that he used to do the calculations. "If I remember correctly, there are five carats to one gram and twenty-eight grams to the ounce. That would make an ounce equal to about 140 carats." Joe looked perplexed which was what Andy had intended him to be. " So if each carat has of an average price of say..." Andy did the calculations in his head so as not to reveal the figure he had in mind, and then deliberately divided the answer by three so that Joe would only be told a figure of about a third of what he had worked out - "so, you might get," he looked at Joe for his reaction, "aboot £30,000."
Joe's eyes opened wide. "Jumping Jehoshaphat" and he gave a long drawn out whistle of disbelief. It was obvious that he had had no idea how Andy had done the calculations, but he had been impressed. Realising that this would probably be his only opportunity to get rid of them, he had to be satisfied with the figure he had been given. "Are you sure that you'll be able to get that amount of dough for 'em?"
Charlie MacKenzie sprang to Andy's mind immediately. "I think I ken a jeweller in Glasgow who'd be interested."
Joe's mind was working fast as he replaced the stones into the bag and put them back into his tunic pocket. "Now just let me think." Joe lit another cigarette and after a few minutes had it figured out. "If you mean what you say, here's what I wan'yer to do," he waited to see if his new friend had an objection. Andy waited to see what he had to say.

"I ain't gonna give yer the diamonds, but first get that price confirmed from yer contact in Glasgow after yer tell him what you've seen. Then, second, when you get up there, book me a room at a small hotel for two - the name of Harrison. That's my girl-friend's name, cos I'll be takin' her with me pretendin' to be on honeymoon. That'll take any suspicion off why we're there, so don't give the hotel any warnin' who'll be comin', except that we're a married couple, okay? We'll follow later on, an' then we don't waste any time in seein' that jeweller friend of yours. I suspect that he'll be making a good profit, so yer can take yer cut from him - I guess they're worth a lot more than yer said, so I'll expect nothin' less than the figure you've given me, okay? Oh, and by the way, make sure yer tell him I'll want cash."

Andy didn't need to think very long about what Joe had said. He was certain that the value of the stones would be at least £120,000 and, when the stones were evaluated correctly, probably a lot more, but he would keep all that to himself. Before he could agree, Joe added, "There's only one condition, an' that is, yer don't ask any questions."

Andy shuddered a little at the thought of what Joe might do if he found out that he had given him such a low figure of their real value, but at the same time, the whole arrangement sounded very suspicious. Why all the secrecy? He was not particularly fond of Americans, and he certainly did not trust this one. It seemed to him fairly obvious that he had deserted his unit after stealing the diamonds. No one in his right mind would have given them to him as he had said, and it sounded too much of a coincidence for the person who had given them to him, if there was one, to be killed soon afterwards. However, because of their true value, he was not going to argue with any conditions that Joe put on the deal, but first, he would like to discover a little bit more about this American.

"There is one question I want t'ask before I agree," Andy said, "and it's nothing to dae wi' the diamonds."

"Fire away," Joe said confidently.

"What are you doin' on this fuckin' hospital ship? You don't appear to be wounded and I dinna believe you're anything to do with the Red-Cross." I tek it yer a deserter, so what are you goin' to do when yer get to England?
The blunt questions took Joe by surprise but he thought he would answer them calmly "I thought yer said you were dern well goin' to ask only one question. I just counted two!"
"A'right then," Andy interjected, "I want to ken what fuckin' risks I'm taking if I agree to help you."
Joe contemplated whether he ought to tell him the truth after all. The Scotsman had said *if* he agreed to help him. Joe could not afford to let this opportunity go by, as it was doubtful whether he would get a better chance than this of getting rid of the diamonds. He hesitated for a while before he said anything, wondering whether he ought to tell a complete stranger the whole story of how he managed to obtain them, but it could be the way to ensure that the Scotsman would help him - so he decided to tell him everything. "Okay, Jock, I'll level with yer, if that's the only way yer going to help me."
Andy cringed. He hated being called Jock, especially by a Yank!
"I stole the diamonds from a jeweller in a small shop in Belgium" Joe began. He waited to see if there was any reaction. There was none. Andy did not flinch. He had dealt with people who brought him stolen goods when he had worked in Glasgow before the war, but he was not prepared for what came next from this unscrupulous American.
"This crafty son of a bitch had kept 'em hidden from the Germans throughout the occupation, an' when I called in to his premises for a small souvenir, it was by chance that he'd just recovered 'em from where he'd had 'em hidden. I couldn't believe my luck as he told me how he had deceived the Bosch, but he refused to give me even a single diamond, so the only way I could get 'em was to bump him off."
He paused and once more waited to see if there was any reaction. Again there was none, so he continued. "I don't believe anybody saw me, and I hoped that when his body was recovered people

would think that he was killed an' robbed by the Jerries before they left. So, my Scottish friend, no one knows about 'em except you, an' no one knows I'm here, right? Does that satisfy yer?"
Andy remained silent as he listened to the American's incredible story, finding it difficult to take it all in.
Joe looked hard into Andy's face. "So what yer gonna do?"
Andy's heartbeat increased considerably as Joe's last remark sounded more like a threat than a question. He tried to ignore it.
"So you're wanted for fuckin' desertion, theft and murder" he said bluntly. "Phew! The people I do business with!" and gave the American a weak smile. He could see that he was dealing with someone who would stop at nothing to get what he wanted.
Andy realised that he would have to be careful. This American had committed one murder, and no doubt would do another if he was forced to, but now that he had been told the truth he had little option but to do as requested. After all, he would make a lot of money in the deal, even though he knew that once he had accepted his role as middleman and seller of the stones, he would then be an accomplice after the fact to Joe's crimes.
Joe was confident that by taking the gamble of telling Andy everything and getting him involved he would ensure the success of his plan. He now felt quite safe and secure in having done so.
"After I've contacted my jeweller in Glasgow, how do I get in touch with you to tell you it's all OK?" Andy asked, "You hinna even given me your full name."
"And yer don't need to know it, my friend. Just Joe will do for now, but you can tell me your jewellers name," and he began writing something down on a piece of paper. "Yer can get in touch with me by callin' this number, and ring me as soon as things are arranged. I want yer to do all this as quickly as possible, OK?' Can you remember everythin' I've told yer?"
The American straightened up and gave Andy the piece of paper he had written on. With his hand firmly gripping Andy's shoulder, added, partly under his breath, "An' I think you'll be fuckin' wise to keep both that telephone number and our conversation to yourself. Okay, Jock?"

Andy took out a packet of cigarettes from his tunic. His hand was shaking as he put one in his mouth and lit it. He fully understood what this American meant but asked courageously, "Can I have anither wee look at those diamonds before you go?"

Joe couldn't wait to get to the Dorset village quickly enough. He was longing to see Liz: to make love to her, show her the diamonds and tell her of his plans to take her to Scotland. He also thought that the village would be the ideal place to stay out of the way waiting for his Scottish confederate to ring.

CHAPTER SIX

From the beginning of May in 1944, Liz never saw or heard from him again until he now suddenly appeared at her cottage door over ten months later.

"I'm back, Honey," he shouted, raising his arms above his head, then closing them tightly around her waist. He was holding a bottle of Bollinger in his hand, which she felt pressing against her back.

"Just wait 'till I get the dern cork out of this," he said, holding the bottle in front of her, "then we'll celebrate in style."

Liz knew exactly what he meant, as he had often used that phrase when he had wanted to make love. After three good glasses of champagne she didn't care. However, it was not quite the same as it had been when they had first met. Even while they were making love she could not stop herself from wondering what he was doing here, and how he had managed to get leave. It seemed strange that no other soldier of any nationality was in the area, as she presumed that they were all still fighting in Germany or wherever. And apart from that, how he had managed to get a passage and acquire that rare bottle of champagne? She assumed that there was no doubt he had stolen it.

Sometime later as they lay together naked on the bed, she pointed to the now empty bottle and asked, "Where did you get that, Joe?"

"Does it matter Honey? Stop worryin'. Anyway, I've gotten something for yer far more interestin' than that bottle of bubbly."

He stubbed out his cigarette in the ashtray by the side of the bed.

She lay there looking at him and fear came over her. She was certain that whatever he was going to show her was going to be the result of something either dishonest or unpleasant. She still had presents that he had brought her previously, her conscience not allowing her to open them suspecting that they had most likely been stolen. When he began telling her not to worry, it usually meant that she would probably need to, so it wasn't hard to guess that she was about to listen to yet another lie.

"Whatever it is that you have, Joe," Liz said quietly, looking into his eyes, "I need to know how you got it, and, while you're at it, you can tell me where the champagne came from as well."
Joe knew that he wouldn't be able to deceive her, but wondered how she would react when he told her that he was not only a deserter, but also wanted for murder.
Liz listened as he unravelled the mystery, her face losing its colour, and she was almost too scared to speak when he had finished his story. He got off the bed and, feeling inside his tunic on the back of the chair, produced the bag of diamonds he had stolen. Without saying another word he tipped the shiny stones on to her bare skin. One settled snugly into her navel.
"My, that looks pretty," he quipped. "You oughta leave it there for ever," and he gave a hearty chuckle, and then kissed her passionately.
"If you're a good girl, half of those are yours," he added, lying back down on the bed beside her.
Liz opened her eyes wide, forgetting for a second how he had come by them, and hardly daring to breathe for fear of spilling all the diamonds off her white-skinned body and on to the bed. She sat up to look at what lay there and asked excitedly, "How much are they worth, Joe?" Then a terrible thought flashed through her mind - was she trying to evaluate them against the life that had been taken?
"Are you ready for this, Liz? At least you won't faint lyin' down."
He paused, mainly for dramatic effect, and then sat up to whisper in her ear, drawing out his words very slowly, "Probably well over one-hundred and twenty-thousand dollars. That's about thirty thousand in your English pounds...and that's fifteen thousand pounds each, honey.
Liz stared at him incredulously, swallowing hard. "You must be joking!" she exclaimed.
"How about that?" Joe said grinning. "They're worth a dern lot more but we'll probably only get less than half their real value. I'm waitin' for a phone call confirmin' the real figure, and soon after that we'll be in the money."

Liz was thoughtful as she got up off the bed and dressed hurriedly without saying a word. Joe had killed for the stones and was also wanted by the Army for desertion. If he got caught it would be no more than he deserved. But fifteen thousand pounds! It was an awful lot of money and it would be all for her. She had never had a real break in her life, and that amount of money would make her rich. If she went along with him, she would never have any more worries. She was certain that Joe would go back to America at his first opportunity after the diamonds had been sold and no one would ever be able to trace where her share of the money had come from. It was an opportunity that came once in a lifetime and, by the time she was dressed, she had decided to go along with whatever arrangements Joe had made.
"When will you find out? How will you get the money?" she asked.
Joe explained that he would have to wait until he heard from a Scotsman he had met on the hospital ship on the way over from Calais. "I'll still be here until that happens, but meanwhile I have arranged to see him at Aldershot. He's in the army and had to first report back there before he leaves for Scotland to get treatment for a shoulder injury. I'll be back in a day, then, as soon as I hear, we'll go to Glasgow to get the cash for the diamonds. So you'll just have to be patient 'till then, honey."
Joe told her that he planned to lie low until the war was over. "Then we could get married and go to the States together as husband and wife."
Quite apart from the difficulties of those arrangements and the fact that it was highly unlikely that it would be possible for Joe to get a passage, Liz wouldn't tell him yet that she had no desire to go with him, for fear of losing out on her share of the money. She decided that she would continue with their relationship, keeping all this to herself until all the arrangements had been completed, then probably go back to London and start a new life there.

For the next week working behind the bar was a very busy time with everyone anticipating joyfully that the war in Europe was

almost at an end. Even Joe wasn't questioned by any of the customers as to why he was there, and was treated as something of a hero by the local population.
It wasn't long before Joe received his telephone call from the Scottish soldier, Andy McKern. Andy told him that the arrangements made were for him to take the diamonds to Charlie MacKenzie's shop in Sauchiehall Street at eight o'clock on the following Wednesday evening. He also confirmed that, subject to a final satisfactory examination, the amount he had estimated for the diamonds would be about right.
Liz could hardly contain her excitement when Joe told her. What Andy didn't tell Joe is that he had made his own agreement with the jeweller to keep an extra four thousand pounds for himself.
Joe guessed that he was being offered far less than they were worth, otherwise the amount would not have been confirmed so easily, but he was more than satisfied with the figure, and was anxious to get rid of the diamonds as quickly as possible.
He told Andy that he and his girl friend would be travelling on the 9.30 train to Glasgow on Friday evening, arriving early next morning. "Where have you booked for us to stay?"
"I've provisionally booked you in the Renfield Hotel in St. Enoch's Square, but I'll confirm it when you get to Carlisle station and I'll meet you in the waiting room and let you know that everything's OK."
Joe decided that he would not tell Liz about his meeting with Andy until they reached Carlisle. The less she knew the better.
However, should anything go wrong, he did tell her about the arrangements that had been made with the jeweller and the location of the hotel where they would be staying.
Meanwhile, Liz had told her boss that she wanted to visit her aunt in Glasgow and would probably stay about a week. She hoped that he didn't mind. When he discovered that Joe too was going to Glasgow on the same train he wondered whether Liz was telling the truth and questioned her. She told him that it was a co-incidence and that she really was going to stay with her aunt. Although Cornelius remained suspicious, he decided not to

question her further. After all, why should she lie? Perhaps she was telling the truth, but it did seem strange that she should be taking the journey so late at night.

She caught a local train to London late in the afternoon, bought her ticket at Euston Station, had a light meal in the station buffet and waited there until she was able to board the overnight express to Scotland. When she did so, she was lucky enough to find an empty carriage and pulled down the blinds. Putting her feet against the door to prevent anyone else from entering, she waited for Joe with breathless excitement.

Going to London was a risk and Joe knew it. Fortunately there were a number of other American soldiers in the City when he arrived on Friday evening. He had put the diamonds in a side pocket of a small army rucksack together with a change of clothes and a few personal items. He had given it to Liz, telling her that he would watch her from a discrete distance until she boarded the train and then he would follow soon afterwards. In that way, they wouldn't be seen together.

When Joe arrived at the station, the Military Police seemed to be everywhere but he avoided them just in case he was stopped and questioned. He waited until it was time for the express to leave, then slipped out of the waiting room on to the darkened platform and boarded the train at the very last minute.

CHAPTER SEVEN

Howard Hartwell stood alone on the almost deserted platform of the small Staffordshire Railway Station. The night was cold for April, and as a fresh easterly wind blew gustily down the line it caused the few travellers waiting for the train to sink their heads into their shoulders and curl up like snails crawling into their shells. He pulled his warm Navy issue overcoat tightly around him to prevent him from feeling the cold. Except for the wind, there was an eerie silence about the place as the people sat quietly on the cold hard metal seats, which were evenly spaced out along the platform.

The powerful express trains frequently made a brief stop at this lonely and desolate place in the Midlands, due to its being one of the few junctions where the Northern line crossed over and above this main route to Scotland from London's Euston Station.

Howard knew that the train journey he was about to undertake would take up many hours of tedious travelling, with the same types of boring people who had been on the train on every previous occasion. He usually found that his fellow travellers were not the best conversationalists and on a long journey he would often fall asleep for most of the way.

Howard always took a book to read, usually one that he had already read or was in the middle of reading. He found that these were easiest for him to able to concentrate on. Combined with the rhythmic sounds of the steel wheels of the carriages passing over the rail joints and junctions, reading a book he had read before often helped to lull him off to sleep.

He looked at his watch, which confirmed that the express was already almost twenty minutes behind its scheduled time. It was not unusual for trains to arrive at Glasgow's Central Station up to three quarters of an hour late, and, because of this, he usually caught this earlier train. After arriving in Glasgow he would then get aboard one of the transport vehicles that would be waiting to

take him and other naval personnel to the Naval Air Station at Abbotsinch.
Five more long minutes went by, before the huge engine arrived at the Midland station, pulling twelve coaches behind it. Its black smoke belching from the funnel as it screeched and squealed to a halt amidst clouds of choking steam, almost blocking out the doors and windows of the train. Carriage doors were flung open; there was banging and shouting then seconds later, more loud clattering as doors slammed shut. A whistle blew and the train jerked away violently, nearly knocking Howard off his feet as he moved down the corridor.
Stooping a little, he peered through the windows of each dimly-lit compartment looking for one with plenty of room. Most seemed to have three or four of those usual boring-looking people on each side, shoulder to shoulder, either staring out of the window, sleeping, reading newspapers, magazines or books. Howard smiled to himself when he saw no-one having a conversation of any kind, confirming his theory that most people lost their ability to converse when travelling on a train. He amused himself with the thought that being English, perhaps they did not speak to one another because they had not been introduced! He had almost decided to squeeze between two rather stout ladies wearing oversized floral hats, one of whom was knitting a scarf which appeared to be already three or four or five feet long, when he noticed that the next compartment's blinds were down.
Hesitating for a moment to decide whether to try the door, he made a noise of falling against it before sliding it partly open. This he thought would warn whoever was inside to stop whatever they were doing - if anything - as he reasoned it highly unlikely that the compartment was full of people. Surely they would hardly have all agreed to the blinds being pulled down if it had been.
In fact there was only one seat occupied, and that by a very attractive girl sitting by the window. She turned to smile as he entered and immediately he could see that she was beautiful. Her long auburn hair was neatly groomed and reached down to her shoulders, but then her expression immediately changed and

looked disappointed, making it obvious that he was not the person she had expected to see come into the compartment.
"Is this anyone's seat?" Howard asked, pointing to the place opposite to where she was sitting. He knew immediately that it had been a stupid question as no one else was in the compartment, but he had to say something and it had been the first thing that had come into his head. He could see that apart from a single suitcase and a rucksack on the rack there was no other luggage. He placed his case alongside it, took off his heavy dark blue greatcoat and placed it on the seat beside him. The carriage was quite warm but if it became colder he could easily put it back on without have to reach up on the rack for it.
The girl hesitated for a second before replying to his question with a shake of her head combined with a slight shrug of her shoulders, giving Howard another brief smile.
She was dressed very smartly in a plain fawn skirt, white jumper and a smart tweed coat that was draped casually over her shoulders. She had one very shapely leg gently resting over the other, her skirt discreetly covering the knee. Howard immediately noticed that she was wearing sheer nylon stockings and came to the possibly unfair, but plainly obvious conclusion, how she had obtained them. He knew that they were almost impossible to find throughout the war years and still were difficult even now in 1945 when it looked as if the end of the war was in sight. Everyone knew that American soldiers could obtain them very easily, and, with uncharitable suspicion, he believed that the American G.Is gave them to the girls in exchange for services rendered.
Howard dismissed the thought as being unkind, not wanting to contemplate that this beautiful girl could possibly be guilty of doing anything as low as that. Furthermore he was feeling the excitement and the luck of finding this lovely travelling companion alone in the carriage, probably on leave from the WACS, which would explain the rucksack. But he wondered whom she had expected to see when he had walked in. He hoped that perhaps it was just a female friend. But why were the blinds of the corridor windows pulled down? Was she really alone and

who was her travelling companion? Howard looked at the one suitcase and the army rucksack on the rack, and wanted them both to belong to her.
The girl was idly flicking through the leaves of "Picture Post," and as the train picked up speed, she began rocking gently with the movement, her hair lightly brushing her cheeks as she turned the pages of her magazine. Would she be going all the way to Glasgow alone as he hoped? He had to ask her to find out.
At that precise moment the door was slid open with a loud thump. The girl came suddenly alive, put down the journal and greeted the tall good-looking American G.I. who quickly entered slamming the sliding door closed behind him.
"You've been a long time, Joe. We've got company. And a sailor at that."
He turned to look at Howard. "Hi, fella. I'm Joe," the tall American said, with a huge grin and holding out his large hand towards Howard.
Howard introduced himself, half getting up off his seat and shook the American's hand.
The G.I. looked back at the girl, and then went very serious for a second, shaking his head almost imperceptibly as he sat down. "No-one there," he said quietly.
"How far yer goin', sailor?" he asked, returning to that same cheerful, bouncy attitude he had shown when he came into the compartment.
"All the way to Glasgow I'm afraid," Howard replied almost apologetically. He immediately wished he had not said it quite like that, as it must have sounded as if he was apologising for coming into the compartment. He was disappointed, however, as he had hoped that the girl's companion would have been female. It would have to be a man - and an American at that. "Damn it!" he said to himself.
Joe laughed perceiving Howard's discomfiture. "Yer needn't be afraid sailor! We ain't goin' to hurt yer," and he laughed again. "Here, have some candy." He threw Howard a bar of chocolate from out of his pocket.

Howard had put his case on the rack but kept hold of the book he had been carrying. He opened it and began to read. The couple whispering quietly disturbed him, and occasionally he caught a word or two of what they were saying. They both appeared to be worried about something at first, and then sat in silence for a while before becoming more relaxed, but engaging in a kind of stifled conversation. The strange relationship between his two companions disturbed Howard's concentration, causing him to read each page over and over again, before eventually settling down to become absorbed in his book. Soon they were at Crewe, and then later, after reading a few more chapters, Howard noticed that they were going through Preston. He slept after that until he awoke to find that the train was almost in Carlisle.

He had begun to stir just before the train stopped, probably being disturbed by his two fellow passengers talking in loud whispers, apparently getting annoyed with each other again and obviously disagreeing about something. She had removed her coat, which she had placed on the seat opposite next to where he was sitting. He glanced in her direction to admire her figure. The well-defined contours of her body reminded him of the beautiful film stars in the American musicals that were popular at the time. He suddenly realised that he was staring but fortunately she appeared not to notice, being absorbed in her argument with the American.
Howard knew that this was going to be a much longer stop as the train always divided here with the front part going on to Glasgow. The rear coaches would be coupled to one of the two engines of the train that would then proceed to Edinburgh. The announcement was repeated many times by the guard as he moved along the corridor to each compartment to ensure that everyone was aware of what was happening and that the passengers were in the appropriate part of the train.
The girl looked scared as the American rose from his seat.
"Be careful, Joe." She held onto his sleeve for a few seconds as she spoke.

"Sure will, honey. Only be a few minutes and I'll be back. Stop worrying." He took the rucksack off the rack and placed it between the girl and the side of the carriage, "Here, look after this while I've gone."
Howard could not help wondering what it was all about. However, Joe was gone an usually long time and the girl began to fidget, continually looking out of the window into the semi-darkness all the while he was away.
Suddenly, there appeared to be a lot of commotion and noise outside and a small crowd of people on the platform were standing still, peering through the semi-darkness towards the front of the train. Then there were loud whistles, the train jerked and began to move forward very slowly. The girl jumped up in alarm and looked at Howard as if asking for help, her eyes wide open like a frightened animal.
"Joe's not back on the train!" she remarked almost hysterically. She looked up towards the communication cord above the window. Howard jumped out of his seat to grab hold of her arm before she could pull the red chain down which would apply the brakes.
"No! No! I'm sure there's no need. He will have got on at the last minute and he'll walk into the..."
Howard stopped what he was saying as they both stared out of the window at the scene outside.

CHAPTER EIGHT

On the dimly lit platform, an American soldier was being led away by two U.S Military Police. They held him tightly by the arms and Liz could just see the side of his face in the semi-darkness. As the train crawled slowly by, Howard and the girl stood motionless for the few seconds it took them to take it all in.
"That was Joe," she said, partly under her breath, and put her hand to her mouth after loudly inhaling.
Instinctively, Howard's eyes looked up towards the communication cord but thought better of it. After all, it was nothing to do with him and in any case there would have been nothing they could have done.
"Oh no!" she gasped, as her eyes filled with tears. She appeared to lose all the air from her body, collapsing back into her seat and looking lifeless, the energy and vitality she had shown earlier now gone.
Howard hesitated before he spoke. "What was all that about? Is he deserter or something?"
The girl began to sob and Howard felt helpless. "What are you going to do now? Can I help in any way?""
She shook her head. "I don't know what I'm going to do," she said drying her eyes with a pretty handkerchief. Her mind was in a whirl. What could she possibly do without Joe.
She felt the rucksack at her side. She had been so looking forward to receiving all that money and now it was more than likely that Joe would be sent back to the United States and she would never see him again. The plans had been made and although Joe had told her what had been arranged, surely the jeweller wouldn't give *her* the money for the diamonds. That apart, even if he would, she couldn't possibly manage the exchange all on her own.
She sat quietly for a while staring out of the window into the pitch darkness. Howard did nothing. He had offered her his help and she hadn't responded. He could see that she appeared to be wrestling with a problem but to ask again if he could help would seem as if he was interfering.

The girl straightened up a little, then, lifting her head, looked straight into Howard's face. She knew that now she would be unable to handle the situation without help from someone. The sailor was her only hope, but could she trust him? He had offered to help her but would it be fair to get him involved with her problem. If she told him what she and Joe were going to do and what was in that rucksack Joe had put by her side before getting off the train, he would probably report her to the police when they got to Glasgow. On the other hand she could tell him part of the story and if she got the wrong reaction from him she could stop before she said anything about the diamonds. She hardly dared contemplate what she would do if he refused to help her but there was no one else she could ask. She had to take a chance.
Howard began to rise from his seat aware that she was about to speak to him and thought that perhaps to sit beside her might make it easier for her if he did so.
"I'm sorry if I was staring at you. Please sit down again where you are. I need someone to help me but I don't know what to tell you."
She lowered her head and looked down at the floor of the carriage. She tried to swallow but her mouth was dry.
Howard sat back down on his seat opposite without taking his eyes off her, patiently waiting for her to continue. He had to admit that he felt excited at the prospect of helping this pretty companion. Her breathing was laboured and it was plain to Howard that her mind was working hard trying to solve her problem.
She looked back up to him trying to decide whether she should go on. Her eyes were clear and beautiful but now without a tear. Howard never took his eyes off her as he waited for her to continue. He was aware that if he began asking her questions he would be involved with whatever was worrying her. But at least he could listen. Then he recalled the whispered conversations she had had with the American - the arguments and sharp exchanges that had taken place, the worried look they both gave when he had first entered the carriage and the concern she expressed when Joe insisted on leaving the train for a while, but then never to return.

As events had proved, she had been right to be concerned, but now it appeared that she was desperate and needed his help.
Had she known what might happen by foreseeing the danger? Howard also thought it strange that the American had given the girl his rucksack to look after if he had only meant to be off the train for a minute or two. And why had he wanted to leave the train in the first place? Howard was suddenly aware that he was still staring at her as he contemplated these questions. He began to feel sorry for the girl who looked as if her world had come to the end. Perhaps he ought to speak first after all.
"Well first, I think you had better tell me why you need me to help you," Howard said calmly.
His attitude gave her confidence, so she decided to tell him some of the story and wait to see what his reaction would be. She stared out of the window again at her own reflection not able to look straight at Howard as she began to speak.
"Now he's been arrested I think that I'd better tell you about Joe." She paused, wondering whether she still ought to go on. "He's a deserter...and he's also wanted by the military police for other offences. I don't know the details but was very worried that he'd be caught. I tried to warn him not to leave the train, but he said that he had arranged to meet a soldier called Andy McKern there. Probably he let Joe down and warned the police. We had seen Military Police on the platform at Euston but he didn't seem bothered about them as he reckoned that they hadn't recognised him, otherwise, he said, they would have stopped him from getting on the train."
She stopped talking and looked at Howard.
He waited for her to continue, but she remained silent. "And that's it?" he asked. "Why d'yer want to stay with him with his record? Are you in love with him? Is that the full story? Where do I come in, and why do you want me to help you?" He asked her that for the second time. "If there is more then you have to tell me everything if you want me to do something for you." He leant forward and gently took her hands into his. They were cold but wonderfully soft.

"There is another thing, and by the way I am not in love with him, but we were going to do something together." She paused for a moment the blood draining from her cheeks and still not sure if she could trust Howard to keep a secret. "But I don't know what you will say when I tell you there is something in his army rucksack that that the police mustn't discover."
It was now Howard's turn to go pale as he realised that he would probably be landing himself in the soup if he got really involved with this girl's problems. At the same time he realised that this lovely creature was in trouble and needed his help. Realising that he was the only person she could turn to, he had to first find out what she was concerned about. Howard suddenly had a worrying thought. If the part about the Military Police was true, they must have known that he had been on the train, so why hadn't they come aboard to make enquiries or look for anything that he might have been carrying and what was in his rucksack that she was carefully guarding and not wanting the police to discover?
The American had left his hat on the seat. Howard looked at it then jumped up and opened the carriage door, which led into the corridor. He was just in time to see two American soldiers with white belts and cap bands entering the next but one compartment.

CHAPTER NINE

Howard closed the door quickly and almost flew back to his seat.
The girl's eyes opened wide. "What's wrong? What have you seen?" she asked almost hysterically.
"I thought so. It's the Military Police. They're examining the train and they'll be asking questions."
The girl quickly put Joe's hat underneath her and tried to cover the rucksack with her body. "Quick, give me my coat to put over it and sit next to me and kiss me."
Howard did not need to be asked twice. Whatever the reasons were why she wanted no one to know that she had known the American, he was not going to miss this opportunity. He moved quickly off his seat in case she suddenly changed her mind, took her in his arms and pressed his lips against hers. Her skin was soft and she smelt heavenly. Almost at once the door opened, and she pulled away from Howard, feigning surprise. For Howard, it had been all too short an embrace.
The soldier stood in the doorway. "Excuse me, lady. We're trying to find where a G.I. was sitting before he got off the train at the last station. Did you see him?"
"You're the only American soldiers we've seen," the girl lied convincingly.
"Those belong to you two?" he asked, looking up to the racks at the two suitcases.
She followed his eyes and replied that the large one belonged to her and Howard said that the other one was his.
"Sorry, to have disturbed you, lady", he said, closing the door.
Howard turned back to the girl. "I think that this is a good time for us to introduce ourselves don't you?"
She took hold of his arms, trying to get out of his grip. "I'm "Elizabeth Harrison, but everyone calls me Liz, and when you tell me who you are, you can go back to your seat." She tried to push him away but he continued to hold her.
"And what if those men suddenly return and find us opposite each other? Won't that look suspicious?"

"Well, alright then, but sit where you are and behave yourself."
He did as she said, but kept hold of her hands. "Is this Ok?" he asked lifting their clasped hands off the seat.
"Oh! alright then," she said, smiling at him and then added, "but you can never trust a sailor."
He told her that his name was Howard Hartwell, stationed at the Naval Station at Abbotsinch, in Paisley. "But you were telling me that you were going to do something together when you got to Glasgow, and what's this mystery about his rucksack that's worrying you? I've told you before. If you want me to help you I must know everything."
She turned her head away from him and looked out of the window once more. Now Howard could see her reflection in the glass She turned back to look at the man she was hoping to be her saviour in a uniform of the Royal Navy.
"I first met Joe," she began, "about six months before he went to France on D. Day." She paused for a moment wondering how much she should tell him. "We became very friendly and he brought me presents: nylons, perfume, make-up, you know all those things that we can't get because of the war but the Americans could. I was flattered and I was young, and I...we.."
"Had an affair," Howard suggested completing the sentence for her.
She nodded. "And then we knew that the build-up of troops and equipment around the New Forest meant that France would soon be invaded, which we soon found out was to be D. Day." She hesitated again before going on. "Well, I thought that I might never see him again, even though he said he would come back for me after the war. I suppose I was sort of in love with him and thought that he loved me too." She looked down at her lap. "But after a while, I began to discover things about him which I didn't like."
"Such as?" Howard asked, trying to sound compassionate.
"His lies. He told me that he'd stolen most of the things he brought me, even boasted about it, but as I didn't want to get him into trouble I said nothing to anyone."

Howard had some questions but thought it better not to interrupt and let her tell her story in her own way.
She suddenly let go of Howard's hand and became frightened. "Oh, Howard...his rucksack! ...We must empty it and then throw it away. If those two Army Policemen come back to make a more detailed search of each compartment when they can't find out which compartment he was in they would they would want to know why we were hiding this rucksack and then discover what's in it. Remember we told them our only luggage was on the rack."
When Liz mentioned about the Police returning it reminded him about their tickets. "Oh hell! I've just thought. If they check our tickets they will notice that you got on in London and mine is from the Midlands. We'll have to be careful of what we say if they question us."
Her eyes were wide open and she looked scared as she picked up his rucksack.
"Why must we empty it? There's still something you haven't told me," Howard said, "You obviously know what's in it."
She went pale, and spoke very quietly. "A lot of money."
"Cash?"
She knew now that she would have to tell him because there was no point keeping it from him any longer but was worried how he would react.
"No.... not money.....Diamonds!"

CHAPTER TEN

Howard put his fingers through his hair and closed his eyes, hoping to find that he had only been dreaming all this. "Oh my God!" he exclaimed. When he opened them again she was still there. "And I'd always imagined that it was only blondes that were dangerous," he added flippantly. "My mother never warned me about girls with ginger hair."
Liz managed a weak smile, the second Howard had seen since Joe left the train at Carlisle.
Then he then thought about what she had said. "We can't do that - we mustn't do anything about his rucksack. I presume that the diamonds are in there?" His beautiful companion nodded. "If they come back with more questions after they find out that no one has admitted seeing him on the train, then they might make a closer inspection of what people are carrying. If they find the rucksack on the seat, they would wonder why we didn't tell them who's it was in the first place, then they'll examine it and discover the diamonds that you say are in it."
Howard was trying in vain to think of another explanation but if they discovered the rucksack they would both be in serious trouble. How the devil did I come to be in this mess? he thought. The girl now looked not quite as pretty as when he first saw her.
Suddenly the door opened again and there stood the other Military Policeman.
"Are you sure you didn't see him?" he asked, looking at them both in turn. He asked the question much more authoritatively than his colleague.
Howard suddenly felt very calm and thought that attack was better than defence. "Perhaps he was in one of the other carriages that have gone to Edinburgh," he suggested.
"Sure. We've thought about that possibility. The guard who was on this train has also gone to Edinburgh and that train is being checked for that as well."

As the door closed, Liz looked at Howard, her eyes and mouth wide open with incredulity. "Now that was quick thinking. Perhaps you are the man to help me."
"Never mind," Howard said seriously. "You're making me think like a criminal." That remark made her smile for the third time. "Look Liz, tell me what happened when you met Joe again." He began to suspect that she was being deliberately evasive.
The girl looked at him for a while before answering his question, wondering how much to tell him. She dropped her eyes and again looked down into her lap. "I suppose I'd better tell you the whole story. She paused before going on. "Joe and I were going to Glasgow to sell the diamonds and share the money, but when I saw Joe being taken away the thought went through my mind that I'd still be able to make myself a fortune, but now I think there's no way that I'll be able to handle all that by myself."
She lifted her head to look at Howard again but he immediately felt somewhat apprehensive about offering to help, suspecting what was in her mind. He now knew that to go along with the way she was thinking would inevitably mean that he would become involved in something that sounded very dangerous.
"Joe came back a few weeks ago," she continued, "and at first it seemed quite normal that he had come back to England on leave, but then he told me what he'd done."
"Had he stolen the diamonds from a house or bank that had been bombed?" Howard asked, allowing her the opportunity to give a plausible explanation.
"Worse than that." Her voice began to break and Howard thought she was going to cry. "He told me that he'd robbed a jeweller in Belgium and had to kill him as he went to sound the alarm." Howard threw his arms up in the air in despair and went back to his seat. Elizabeth ignored his gesture and continued. "Then he told me a long story of how he came back on a hospital ship with the wounded, but I didn't take much notice of what he was saying as I was thinking all the while what a terrible thing he had done." She paused and then added, "Then he showed me the diamonds, and I forgot about that poor Belgian."

"He’s wanted for murder then?" Howard said, stating the obvious. "I would have thought that there was no doubt that the Military Police were waiting for him at Carlisle to arrest him. "Why did he risk getting off there?"
"He told me that he had planned to meet a soldier called Andy McKern who he'd met on the boat, to confirm the arrangements of our stay in Glasgow, but I warned him that it might be risky and I was right." Her voice croaked a little and she put her handkerchief to her eyes to dry her fresh tears.
Howard wondered if it might help to express his thoughts.
"I don't think that the police knew about the diamonds because if that had been the case, why didn't they stop the train from leaving and make the search then? And then again, if they didn't know what he was carrying, they possibly didn't know about the murder either, so perhaps they have just arrested him for desertion. There seem to be a lot of questions that need answering."
"But as he hadn't got any luggage with him, that's why they were looking for it on the train, as well as anyone who might have been travelling with him," Liz said, thoughtfully. "But if he was only arrested for desertion, just looking for his luggage wasn’t important enough to stop the train leaving, was it? But if they had known about the diamonds they would have searched the train until they found them, as you said."
Howard nodded. "I believe that they were just trying to find out if anybody was travelling with him."
They sat back in their seats satisfied with the conclusions they had reached.
Howard suddenly had a thought. "When the M.Ps contact each other after these trains arrive at their destinations, things might change very quickly, but there's no point in worrying about that."
He reached over and picked up her coat. "So what do we do with this rucksack? Leave it here or throw it out of the window?" He got up from his seat and began strutting about the carriage nervously. "Or perhaps we could empty it and hide it under the seat or just leave it here after we take out the diamonds." As he sat down again he was beginning to feel scared of what might happen

if it all went wrong. He then had second thoughts. "Why bother, you could take it off with you."
Liz leaned forward as she took hold of his hands and spoke very quietly. "Nobody knows the diamonds are here and I know where Joe was taking them. He was going to get a lot of money for them. What's to stop us from doing what he was going to do and keeping the cash for ourselves?"
Howard couldn't believe what she was saying. She appeared to be so cool about it all.
"Do you know what you are saying, Liz?" Howard's mouth felt dry and his words came out staccato.
"Joe told me that the diamonds were very valuable and he'd been offered about £30,000. Although he believed that it was far less than what they were worth. We could both be rich if we shared it out between us," she said slowly and deliberately.
Blimey! What I could do with £15,000! Howard thought to himself, but what she was suggesting was preposterous.
"No one knows we have the diamonds," Liz said quietly, as if reading his thoughts, "and I don't believe Joe would tell anyone even if he has been arrested."
"How did you both get on the train at Euston?" Howard asked. "Someone must have seen you together." He didn't wait for her to answer but decided to tell her what he'd been thinking. "Perhaps the police did know Joe was carrying diamonds, and you'll be caught red-handed when they look inside people's luggage. They purposely didn't inspect the luggage on the train, because if they had, you could have said you were innocent. That's it! They'll get you when you carry his rucksack through the barrier." He knew now that to succeed with her plan was impossible. "So there's no way we can get away with it," Howard concluded.
She was smiling at him. Why was she smiling, he wondered? What had he overlooked?
"Firstly," she began, "Joe deliberately waited until the very last minute before getting on to the train as it was beginning to move. I was watching very carefully from my seat to make sure that nobody followed him. Secondly, he'd been very careful to ensure

that we were not seen together on the platform and you are the only one who saw him on the train. Thirdly, and most importantly, I'm not going to be carrying the diamonds when we get off the train - you are!"

CHAPTER ELEVEN

Now Howard was convinced that she was not as innocent as she was making out to be. She had planned this trip very carefully with Joe and even had an important role to play herself. She was so obsessed with cashing in on the illegal transaction that even Joe's arrest was not going to deter her from still carrying out the plans they had made. Indeed, it had made it easier for her. The only difference, Howard now began to realise, was that instead of Joe and her, it was going to be him and her. Howard looked into her beautiful face and saw hardness for the first time. Her bright green eyes were now duller in colour. They were cold calculating eyes. The sparkle had gone.

"First we can make sure that no one is waiting at the barrier and then we'll meet later." She paused and then added, "Just think, £15,000 for just carrying a rucksack!" She gave him a radiant smile and squeezed his hand. Her eyes were sparkling again, but Howard's heart was thumping hard inside his chest, and he had sweat on the palms of his hands.

"If you joined up with the other sailors getting off the train, I'm sure that no one would stop you," she told him firmly.

Howard shook his head in case he was dreaming. Perhaps he'd wake up from this nightmare. He opened the rucksack. Inside were items of Joe's personal possessions, toiletries including the usual items for shaving, some underclothes and a shirt. There was also a bulging sealed envelope wrapped up in tissue paper in one of the side pockets.

"The stones are in there," she said.

With the envelope containing the diamonds in his hand and the £15,000 in his head, Howard now began to think more clearly. "There's no way that I could carry this rucksack off the train. Whoever saw a sailor carrying an army rucksack! Sailors carry kitbags. You could take the rucksack off the train with you pretending it was yours and you could put some of yours into it. I could just about squeeze a couple of his things into my case, the toiletries and things like that. Remember that the M.Ps didn’t ask

about it because they didn’t see it, and, if they examined it now you could easily explain that the man’s items are your boyfriend's and that wouldn’t arouse suspicion if the clothes were a mixture of yours and his.
"And what about the diamonds?" Liz sounded concerned.
Now realising that there would be no alternative but for him to carry the diamonds, he tried to reassure her they would be quite safe. "I'll carry the package in the inside pocket of my greatcoat, so that even if my case was examined it would be highly unlikely that my clothing would be searched. In any case, why should they be looking for diamonds? I still think that your friend Joe was arrested for being a deserter."
With the exchanges complete Howard closed the cases and returned them to the rack, then sat back in his seat contemplating the situation. "Do you think it'll work?" he said tentatively.
"Now I've thought about it again, I'm certain it will work," she said clearly and calmly.
Howard still felt some panic, but she looked very cool he thought, but then why shouldn't she? - she wouldn't be carrying the diamonds!
"When will you be able to get away to meet me?" she asked.
He told her that he didn't know exactly, but it may not be until the middle of next week. He would obviously be giving her the diamonds outside the railway station, but how did he know that he would ever see her again? How could he guarantee that she would not just disappear afterwards?
"Arrangements have been made to meet the dealer next Wednesday, but I think that it will be too risky for you to give me the diamonds after we leave the train," Liz explained as if recognising his fears. "You'd better keep them and I'll contact you after the weekend when I've found out that everything is okay to go ahead. If I suddenly hear from Joe then I'll come and see you immediately before he finds out that you have the diamonds"
"But I thought that I was only just going to......" Howard began. Liz interrupted him by putting a finger to his lips. "Ssh! Don’t

change things now. It will work as long as we keep to the plans we've made."
"Where will you stay?" he asked, worried in case she didn't get in touch with him again for some time.
"Oh that was all arranged by Joe. It's the Renfield hotel in St. Enoch's Square, but I'll have to make some excuse for him when I get there."
It all seemed very complicated to Howard, but Liz sounded confident that she could deal with it, so he asked no more questions. Nothing else was said for a long time as the train sped on its way to its destination.

They both stared out of the window watching the sky becoming brighter as the orange sun, slowly began to rise above the dark grey rolling hills of the Scottish Lowlands, the light contrasting with the deep shadows of the valleys and the changing landscape.
Howard felt exhausted, and pulled down the window blind to cut out the light. He felt shattered, not only through lack of sleep but because all the events of the night had sapped his energies. He looked across to where Liz was sitting: her eyes were closed as she tried to catch a few moments sleep before the train reached its destination. She looked beautiful. If only all this hadn't happened, he could easily have fallen in love with her. She was obviously a girl with passions and he fantasized about making love to her before he too fell into a light sleep.
They awoke at about the same time and Howard put the blinds back up on both the outside and corridor windows to make it appear that they were just ordinary passengers and not accomplices to a diamond smuggler, murderer and deserter, even though they had seen the real criminal arrested. Howard reminded himself that he was now also a receiver of stolen goods and even when he had given them back to Liz and received the large sum of money he had been promised, he knew that he would still think of himself as a criminal, albeit a wealthy one.
As soon as the train began to slow down they put on their coats and deliberately made quite a show of their parting for the benefit

of anyone watching. They kissed in the corridor and shouted their goodbyes loudly before Howard put his head out of the window to watch the train sliding alongside the station platform. No one was waiting at the barriers except a solitary railway official.
Howard jumped off the train almost before it had stopped and hurried towards the barrier, carrying his own small attaché case and with his greatcoat buttoned up tightly around him to protect the packet of diamonds in his inside pocket. He joined up with the other servicemen, including sailors from his camp, and hurried past the ticket collector, handing him his ticket. Howard glanced back and saw the two M.Ps running along the platform to the barrier but he was well past before they reached it. Looking back he saw the people queuing as the MPs began their check of the passengers. He hoped that Liz would be alright.
He looked up at the station clock and saw that the train had arrived over half an hour late. All the Navy personnel were rushing to get outside where a truck was waiting to take them to the Naval Air Station at Abbotsinch. Moments later, in the cold air of that early hour, and, seated on the wooden benches in the covered wagon, they were trundling along the empty road to Paisley, Howard felt nervous, aware of the bulge in the inside pocket of his greatcoat, knowing that he would not be happy until he had actually arrived safely in the camp, and able to put the package away and out of sight.

CHAPTER TWELVE

On the journey to Glasgow Joe had got off the train at Carlisle as he had previously arranged to do, joining in with the other passengers on the platform so as not to be too conspicuous. He then made his way to the waiting room to meet Andy, whom he found sitting in a dimly-lit corner looking worried.
"Have you seen the fuckin' Military Police?" were his first words to Joe, "There's a few of them aboot the station hidden away, watching everyone going on and off the train."
"I didn't see any of 'em on the platform, but there were a couple of sons-of-bitches at Euston I had to avoid." Joe sounded concerned. "Maybe I'll have to be careful when I get back on the train. Are all the arrangements the same as yer told me?" he asked, "and you've confirmed the hotel booking."
It was the main reason why Joe had wanted to see the man who had fixed everything for him in Glasgow as he did not want anything to go wrong at the last minute. Andy assured him that the arrangements he had made still stood. Joe waited a few more minutes, looking out continually to see if the platform was clear before he ventured out to return to the train, when suddenly there was a commotion. He saw two M.Ps running across the platform towards one of the carriages blocking his way back. There was a lot of shouting and the few people left on the platform were standing still, watching whatever was happening.
"What's going on?" Andy asked.
"I don't know, but maybe yer ought to go and have a look before I make a dash for it to get back on the train."
Andy went outside but returned after a little while. "The place is full of fuckin' Military Police, and it looks as if two of them have just arrested an American soldier who put up something of a struggle. You'll be seen if you go now - unless you want t'risk it."
Joe hesitated too long before making a decision. He heard a whistle blow and realised that the train was about to leave. If he ran out now, he thought, he would be noticed, and certainly recognised by his uniform as an American soldier. Possibly they

would think that he was an accomplice of the one who had been arrested. He decided that he would not risk it.
"Oh, what the hell! I've left the diamonds in my rucksack. I'll have to stay here until the morning, Andy, and catch an early train tomorrow. Liz'll soon realize I've missed the bloody train, and wait at the hotel until I turn up.. She knows where we're staying."
Joe was convinced that he had nothing to worry about. "When will I see you."
If I can get away, I'll try to see you at the hotel sometime later this morning but then I'll have to return here 'til Thursday when I'm due to go to the hospital in Glasgow to get this bloody arm fixed.

When Joe arrived in Glasgow, he went straight to the hotel, saw the desk clerk, and asked which room Mrs Harrison was in.
"What was the name again, sir?"
"Harrison."
The clerk looked through the book. "I'm sorry sir, but we don't have a Mrs Harrison staying here. That name has been deleted and a Mr and Mrs Hartwell have taken the room. Do you know why it was cancelled sir?"
Joe was completely taken aback by this. "I've no idea. I had arranged to meet her here. When was it done? Would it have been Mrs Harrison?" Joe gave him a full description of Liz.
"I'm afraid I don't know sir, and I haven't seen the person you described. This must have happened before I came on duty."
Joe sat down on one of the easy chairs and ordered a coffee. A Mr and Mrs Hartwell! he had said. This couldn't be Liz, so where could she be? If she had cancelled the room reservation why had she done it? Had she gone back home and where was his rucksack and the diamonds? He could ask the clerk who had been on duty at the time, but he would have to wait until later that day or the next morning.
Meanwhile he would book a room in the name of Mitchell, avoiding his real name of Peabody, and wait to see if she turned up. Surely she would assume that he would arrive sometime today after missing the train. He could also check with the jeweller in

case she tried to sell the diamonds without him, but that would be ludicrous for her to do so. In any case the appointment had been made for next Wednesday and she knew that, and today was only Saturday!
Joe suddenly realized that he had nothing but the clothes he stood up in. He had left his rucksack containing the rest of his things with the diamonds on the train and he needed to get them back from Liz, but where was she? After making various enquiries, he left the hotel to go and buy some personal items, and anything else he thought he would require for the one night. Surely Liz would turn up soon, he thought, dismissing any previous conjectures about her non-appearance.
Joe began to feel more certain that it must have been Liz who had cancelled their booking and when he returned to the hotel, he thought that it would be a good idea to check with the Hartwells to see if they had seen her, and whether she had given them any reason for cancelling their reservation.
He asked the desk clerk if the Hartwells were in the hotel.
"I've checked the room sir, but there doesn't appear to be either of the Hartwells in at the moment." He sounded almost apologetic, although he looked at Joe somewhat suspiciously.
Sometime later as Joe sat reading a newspaper in the foyer, he was astounded to hear Liz's voice asking for her room key. She was alone but she made no enquiry about whether an American G.I. had arrived. So she had a room here after all, but which? He thought that he would wait to see what she did, so he hid behind his paper until she had gone to the lift, and then went over to the desk.
"Mrs Hartwell has just arrived, sir," the clerk informed him.
"Oh yeah? Was that her?" Joe could hardly believe what he had been told. "Has Mr Hartwell come in too?" he asked innocently.
"I understand that he is in the Royal Navy, sir, and will be joining her later."

Joe thought deeply about the situation as he walked back to where he had been sitting. So that was it. It must be that sailor who had

travelled with them in the same compartment. It couldn't have been anyone else. How did they think they would get away with whatever they were plotting? Surely they knew that he would turn up. If they were planning to steal the diamonds that he had left on the train, why had she not gone to another hotel? What made her so certain that he would not be coming here? He then remembered the incident on Carlisle station and the arrest of the American soldier. Maybe they saw the G.I. being taken away by the Military Police and assumed it to have been him. He concluded that that must be the only explanation possible.
Now it all fitted together. Joe suddenly recalled the sailor's name as being Howard. He walked back to the desk. "Can I have another look at the reservations book? Do'yer mind?"
The desk clerk turned it round so that he could read the names. 'Mr and Mrs H. Hartwell.' Joe felt angry "H" Hartwell. That must "H" for Howard. It was obvious that they were going to keep the appointment with the jeweller and keep the money for themselves. So now the situation had changed He decided that he would keep out of sight and see what developed.
That fuckin' son-of-a-bitch sailor has soon stepped into my shoes, he said to himself, and only hours after he thought that he had seen me arrested! He reminded the clerk that he had booked a room for the one night under the name of Mitchell and now wished to stay until at least Wednesday.

He kept out of sight and by the next morning he had worked out a plan. He saw Liz go out on Sunday morning and was about to follow her, when Andy walked into the hotel.
"Am I glad to see you!"
Andy looked surprised. "Why? What's happened?"
"You'll never believe it. But first, why didn't you come here yesterday? I would have thought that you would have come to see how Liz has coped when I didn't turn up."
"Have you forgotten I'm in the army? I'm nae the same as you. I can't come and go as I please. This is the first chance I've had, and this bloody shoulder is giving me jip. Why? What's up?"

"Well I'm glad you've turned up now, because you'll never believe what's happened
"What?"
"Well first I haven't got the diamonds! Liz has, and she doesn't know I'm here."
Andy tried to speak. "Wait," Joe said putting his hand over Andy's mouth.
Joe explained to him what he thought Liz was up to. "After seeing the American arrested on Carlisle station I believe that she thought that was me and got the sailor involved who was in the same carriage and together it looks as if they are planning to keep the money for the diamonds themselves.
"Bloody hell!"
"I think she went out yesterday to look for MacKenzie's shop, and I guess they are going to go there on Wednesday night as you arranged for me to do, but I've worked out a plan to stop them from getting their hands on the money. It'll serve her right, but for the moment I'm keepin' it to myself. I'm goin' to visit your Charlie MacKenzie in the mornin' and explain to him what I want him to do. But, most important, she mustn't know that you've been here. So, fuck off 'til Thursday mornin' and I'll see you then before you go into hospital.
"I just don't see why yer goin' to all this trouble. Why not just show yourself and take the diamonds off her while she's here in the hotel?"
"And if she says she hasn't got them, or that her sailor boyfriend has them, what then? I don't know when he's comin'. My way will guarantee two things. First that the diamonds will get to the shop, and second, I want to see her face when she gets fuck all."
"I dinna mind what you do so long as my fuckin' money's safe," Andy said, laughing.

CHAPTER THIRTEEN

Over the weekend Howard scanned the newspapers in the camp library to look for a report of an arrest of a G.I deserter at Carlisle Station, and what might have happened to the American, but there was nothing. He concluded that it had not been worth a news item as it was commonplace for soldiers to be arrested for being absent without leave, and in any case the papers were full of the latest news of the war in Europe.

The weekend had seemed like an eternity but for the next two days he was busy most of the time in one of the hangars doing 'Daily Inspections' on both Sea-Fire and Firefly aircraft. But at night he lay awake contemplating what he and the pretty "sea-bird" with ginger hair that he had met on the train were going to do. At Tuesday lunch-time he received word from a colleague that there was a girl at the guardhouse asking to see him. His informant described her lovely red hair, which left him in no doubt as to who it was. He had just returned from the hangars on the other side of the airfield. Although still in his overalls he went to meet her,. She looked lovely standing there and gave him a sweet smile.

"You haven't heard anything from Joe then?"

"No and I'm not likely to now he's been arrested. I talked to a British Officer who's in the hotel about what happens to American deserters, and he told me that the army treats the offence very seriously and that more than likely they would be sent straight back to America to serve a prison sentence."

"So you think we are pretty safe then to go ahead?"

"I'm certain. Can you get a pass-out until tomorrow morning from say 5 o'clock today, or as soon as possible afterwards. Bring the diamonds, of course, because we have things to do."

It was short notice but he said that he thought he would be able to arrange that. She told him where to meet her and by five o'clock he had obtained leave to go 'Ashore' for twelve hours. Actually, it took effect straight away but he had to be back in camp by 8 a.m. next morning.

He met Liz who had been waiting for him in the cafe in the Square as she had arranged. As they sat down at a small table covered with a beautifully embroidered tablecloth he felt her hand touch his. He again thought how lovely she looked with her hair shining in the lights of the cafe. He took out the brown envelope containing the diamonds from the inside pocket of his greatcoat.
"Have you had a look inside?" she asked as he handed it to her.
From the look he gave her she could tell immediately that he hadn't opened the package, but Howard was more interested to know what had happened at Central Station after he had left. He remained silent as the waitress brought the pot of tea, which Liz must have ordered as soon as she saw him coming. Howard noticed that she too had ginger hair and the whole of her pretty face was completely covered in freckles. She would have been only a few years younger than the girl sitting opposite him, but compared with her she looked so innocent, and Howard guessed that her life wasn't anywhere near as complicated as that of the girl at his table.
"Did they search your luggage?" he asked anxiously when the young girl had left.
"There were a number of soldiers including two G.Is. that they took to one side, but I don't know what happened to them. The two Military Policemen that we saw on the train questioned some of the other passengers, but I don't think they examined any of the suitcases people were carrying. When it came to my turn they just smiled at me, asked about you, then said what a lucky fella' you were."
Howard laughed, thinking if only they knew how accurate their comments had been.
"But I have something else to tell you which worried me at first" Liz said "and it's also why I haven't contacted you earlier."
Howard waited anxiously for what she was about to say. She paused, appearing to try and find the right way to tell him what was concerning her.
"What have you found out?"

"I went to the hotel in St. Enoch's Square where Joe said he had booked a room. When I got there I found that they were expecting a Mr and Mrs Harrison, which is my name of course. Apparently, the room had been booked in March by a soldier who must have been the one Joe went to meet on Carlisle Station. Fortunately the soldier didn't tell them that Joe was an American G.I., so I told the booking clerk that it was all a mistake, and that he had booked the room in my maiden name of Harrison instead of my husband's name of Hartwell, the name of the man I married a few days ago."
She hesitated for a moment and looked at Howard expecting some reaction from him. There was none. Perhaps he hadn't heard what she had said, so she continued to say what happened.
"I explained that you were in the Fleet Air Arm and that you had to report back to the station at Abbotsinch but that you will be joining me later in the week. That's today."
Howard wasn't really listening. He was worrying about that soldier and what might go wrong. "Are we sure that there is no possibility of your Joe turning up?"
"He is not my Joe, Howard, but I have already explained to you how can he turn up now he's been arrested? That British Officer I told you about, put my mind at rest when he said what happens to deserters. So stop worrying. He did ask me why I wanted to know. That took me by surprise and I had to think quickly so I made the excuse that I had a sister who had had the problem and I was worried about her. He told me that his advice was to tell her to drop the fella like a ton of hot bricks."

While Liz was talking Howard suddenly realised what she had told the desk clerk at the hotel and his eyes opened wide. He could not believe what she had said about being married. It might have been best for her to make up a story, but surely she didn't expect him to turn up at the hotel as her husband!
"Good God! Fancy telling the clerk at the hotel that we're married. What do we do now?"
She was giving him a broad smile and he thought again how beautiful she looked. Her skin was smooth and without a blemish,

her eyes sparkled and she had just the right amount of lipstick to complement the colouring of her well-groomed red hair. Howard knew that he would have gone along with almost anything that she suggested up to a point, but what she said next was caused him to worry.
"Will you come back to the hotel with me now?" She lifted her eyes and stared into his. "I believe that they are beginning to think that I haven't got a husband."
"You haven't," he said, raising his eyebrows, and then suddenly fearing that he might have lost an opportunity added, "but perhaps you don't have to ask twice for me to act like one."
He reached across the table and took her hand into his. It was a gentle hand, warm and soft. He noticed that on her left hand she was wearing a gold ring on her wedding finger. It took him by surprise and looked at her about to ask the question. She anticipated what he was going to say.
"It was only cheap, but I had to get something or people wouldn't have believed us." She was looking at him with those clear green eyes. He dared not ask what he hoped was on her mind. It was certainly on his. But then he thought about Joe's accomplice.
"What about this soldier, McKern, he's........"
Liz stopped him in mid-sentence. "I thought that you'd be worried about him, but that's another reason why I waited for a few days before contacting you."
"But didn't Joe get off at Carlisle to meet him?"
"Yes, I think he did, but if that Scotsman had got on to our train, after seeing Joe arrested, he then would have either looked for me on the train in the belief that I had the diamonds, or come to the hotel to see me knowing that Joe couldn't turn up. I've kept my eyes open and although it's possible that I could have missed him no one has asked for me since I've been here. I don't know what he looks like, of course, and he has never ever seen me. If he *has* called in and checked the register then he would have found that the booking had been cancelled and would have assumed that I had not arrived for whatever reason. He would think it more than likely that Joe had had the diamonds on him when he was arrested

and it was in his best interests to disappear, for obvious reasons. My belief is that Joe befriended him on the hospital ship, gave him some money to book the room and fix the meeting with the jeweller he knew and that's it. He just went to see him at Carlisle close to where he was stationed to see if the arrangements still stood."

She was not to know, of course, that he and Joe had met in the hotel on Sunday morning.

"You seem to have worked it out well and thought of everything, Liz." Howard's worries seemed to be over. He had given her the diamonds and now all he could think of at this moment was that he was going to spend the evening with her, and, get back earlier than he had expected.

She leant forward and spoke in a very quiet voice, "But I'm afraid I do have a disappointment for you..."

He knew it. He thought it too good to be true, then suddenly he remembered the way she had pushed him away in the railway carriage after he had kissed her. She had used him then and now she was going to use him again.

"The desk clerk gave me a letter this morning addressed to Mr Harrison remembering that the room had originally been booked in my maiden name so he thought it was for you. I read it, of course. It was from the jeweller..."

She looked quickly about her to see if anyone was listening to their conversation but there were only a few people in the cafe and Howard was the only man. All the other ladies were busy concentrating on their own small talk. Perhaps there wasn't going to be any money in it for him after all. It had all been a ruse on her part to get him to take the diamonds off the train. He waited for the punch line.

"...he has reduced his offer to £25,000," she continued, "so that's only £12,500 each instead of £15,000."

Howard's eyes opened wide and he didn't know what to say. "Only £12,500", she had said. Oh, my God he thought, only £12,500! Who cares? I'll still be rich.

"He also confirmed that it is tomorrow night when we see him. At eight o'clock he will have taken them off our hands. Meanwhile - you can have a bonus now to celebrate our good fortune." She had chosen that word "celebrate" deliberately, hoping that Howard would recall what she told him Joe had meant when *he* said it.

She leant forward and squeezed his hands together inside hers. Howard grinned. Although to celebrate was something to look forward to and be excited about Howard suddenly felt very nervous about taking the American's place; perspiration was beginning to form on his brow and the palms of his hands were sweating. He hadn't really been listening to all that Liz had said, but she had just mentioned something about him collecting his bonus.

"A bonus?" he asked. "What do you mean, a bonus?"

"You've earned it, Howard." She was smiling at him. "You don't have to be back until morning do you?"

Liz noticed that his cheeks had turned a bright red, and, as they left the cafe he could not remember whether he had finished his tea or not. Cis and Lil, two local prostitutes of an uncertain age, well- known and often talked about by some of the lads in the camp, were standing at the corner close to the bus stop. They never took their eyes off Howard's beautiful companion as they walked by, then laughed together at their own private joke. He had previously felt little envious of some of the lads at the camp who had been out with them, but now he thought how repulsive they both were. Paisley also had a profusion of pretty girls mostly employed at the local textile factory, but he knew that he had a girl at his side more beautiful than any of them.

She was a girl who he had met only a few days before, who was carrying in her handbag a packet of diamonds worth thousands of pounds, soon to be exchanged for cash, which would make them both more wealthy than they could have dreamed about at their age. Was this really happening to him? If it was, them he would have to start to make plans

First he would have to get out of the Navy as soon as he was able and ask her if he could join her wherever she wanted to go.
Howard was very quiet as they waited for the bus to arrive, wondering how on earth he had got himself mixed up in all this. Should he be going along with what they were doing? After all, the diamonds had been stolen and what was worse, Joe had admitted killing the person who he'd stolen them from. They were not only handling stolen goods but were accomplices in the crime that had been committed.
Liz squeezed his hand as if she was reading his thoughts and looked at him.
"Howard. What else could we do if we don't go ahead with what we've planned?"
"We could hand the diamonds over to the police and tell them all about Joe."
"And what do you think they will do to us after keeping quiet about it all? We haven't done anything wrong apart from that. Stop worrying. Let's just take the money and disappear. No one will ever know."
Howard looked at the girl. Her face radiant, and looking even more beautiful than before.
Perhaps she was right, thought Howard. No one could ever discover who was the owner of the jewels and, in any case, he was dead - killed by Joe, so should he stop worrying and first enjoy the moments that lay ahead before seeing the jeweller tomorrow evening?
He was looking forward to the company of this young lady who he could easily fall in love with. If she felt the same way, it would be an opportunity not to be missed and they would have a start in life with a wealth that many people would envy.
They boarded the bus when it arrived and Howard handed the money for the tickets to the conductor, not really aware of how much he had given him or whether he had received any change. His thoughts being elsewhere

CHAPTER FOURTEEN

For Howard, the bus seemed to take an interminable time to arrive in Glasgow, picking up at every stopping place on the journey. When they eventually arrived at the hotel Liz slipped her arm through Howard's as they approached the reception desk. After she gave her room number, the clerk handed her the key and greeted Howard with a cheery, "Good evening, Mr Hartwell."
Howard was taken completely by surprise but it gave him the assurance that no one would know that they were not married. "I'm beginning to feel that I am married to you after all," he whispered as they walked away from the desk..
"You must be pleased that Mr McKern hadn't said that you were an American, otherwise you'd have had to hire a G.I's uniform and put on an American accent." She laughed, and then added, "Aren't you lucky?"
Howard certainly had to agree to that, but for a completely different reason from the one she had given.

An hour or so later they had a wonderful romantic meal in the restaurant. She wished that she still had that bottle of champagne that Joe and she had shared on the bed in her room when he had first showed her the diamonds but she wasn't going to tell Howard that. They followed the meal with a large glass of Scotch whisky that the hotel had somehow conjured up, no doubt thinking that they were on their honeymoon. The Head Waiter gave them a knowing smile as they left the dining room, which also confirmed what the misinformed staff must have assumed. The thought went through Howard's mind that the cost of the meal didn't matter as he knew that he would have plenty of money to pay the hotel bill on the Thursday morning before they left.

Next day he awoke early to find himself lying in the most luxurious bed he could have imagined, alongside the most beautiful girl he could ever have dreamed about. He wanted to make love to her again there and then, but knew that the clock

prevented him from doing so. Their clothes were scattered all over the floor and Howard smiled when he remembered the trouble that they both had had trying to remove his uniform the night before. The tight fitting 'top' of the 'square rig' traditional Navy uniform was always difficult to remove in normal circumstances, usually having to be pulled inside out over the head of the wearer, but after all that alcohol and the desire to remove their clothes urgently, it had caused all sorts of problems, until eventually they had both ended up practically in hysterics.
The smile left his face as he looked again at his watch, realising that he had only just enough time to get back to the camp. It was almost six-thirty. It would take him about an hour to return to the camp. He had first to catch a tram to Paisley and then walk about a mile and a half to the entrance. He also knew that if Liz was wide awake he would never be able to get back on time. So he slipped out of bed quietly, dressed hurriedly, then went over to the bed to kiss his 'newly wed wife' goodbye. She looked so peaceful and contented and even more beautiful without any make-up. He hesitated for a moment before kissing her gently on the lips.
"Thanks for the bonus," he whispered as she opened her eyes. "I'll get here as quickly as I can tonight, and after we've seen this jewellery bloke tomorrow, what about some more bonuses?" he asked flippantly.
"Only if you're a good boy," she said, flinging her arms around his neck, kissing him passionately.
Howard dragged himself away telling her reluctantly that there was no time. "I must go and if I'm late I won't be able to get leave this evening." He left the room hurriedly not daring to look back.

The day seemed interminably long and Howard couldn't stop thinking about the night before. The diamonds were now only his second thoughts. He did not care if they only got a few pounds for them. The thrill of being with her was enough. He still wasn't happy about meeting this dealer or diamond merchant whatever he was and he was worried if Joe would still turn up at the last minute. He was aware that he was involved with a bunch of

crooks and was concerned about the risk they were going to take, but he told himself that the money would compensate him for all the worry.
Although Howard knew nothing about the value of diamonds, it seemed strange to him that the price had apparently been agreed without the buyer ever having seen the goods. It was something that shouldn't be of concern to him really but it put a little doubt in his mind that things might not go as planned.
Another thing playing on his mind was after they had received the money in exchange for the diamonds how would he explain his own sudden rise to riches?
The Scottish soldier she had talked about also worried him. Where was he? Had Joe already paid him for making the arrangements, and what else did he know? Howard pushed all of these questions to the back of his mind and thought of Liz. Would she go straight back home after she got the money? He could not bear to think that he would not see her again. He just wanted to hold her in his arms and feel her warm body next to his and to make love to her.

He left the camp about five o'clock and got a lift to Glasgow in a station wagon arriving at the hotel about half an hour later.
She was waiting in her room and appeared a little nervous.
"I've looked at the diamonds. They're beautiful," she said. "I just had to open the package and I've taken two of the biggest ones out."
She passed one over to Howard. "Here - one each. I don't think the jeweller will notice. Joe told me that he thought that his offer is way below the real price he should be paying for them anyway, and, apart from that, he hasn't even seen them yet."
"What are we going to do?" Howard asked. "We have a lot of time to spare." He wanted to make love to her.
"Let's eat," she said.

CHAPTER FIFTEEN

Howard felt a pang of disappointment when she suggested having a meal instead but when they returned with the money they would have the whole night ahead of them. He began to fantasise about making love to her with ten-pound notes covering her naked body. They ordered the best meal on the sparse but adequate menu, starting with game soup, followed by poached salmon and Hollandaise sauce and baked apple for sweet. As there was no wine obtainable, they drank a couple of large gin and tonics with their meal.

"I think it's time we left," Howard suggested as he looked at the clock in the restaurant. It was showing twenty minutes to eight. He gave her a warm smile "Hope you've got the package safe?" Howard thought that she looked particularly ravishing. He called the waiter and signed the bill. Again it looked a lot of money for a meal for just two people, more than he was paid in a month in the Navy, but he didn't care. Money didn't matter. He would soon be rich.

They walked out of the hotel and through St. Enoch's Square into Union Street, then continued along Renfield Street. It was a cold evening for April and the wind cut right through their outer garments as they approached Sauchiehall Street. It had taken them longer than they thought, the clocks having struck eight o'clock long before they had reached the tiny premises of the jeweller's shop. There was a sinister atmosphere about the area as they went round the corner of a little side street to knock on the back door of the building. It was fortunate that Liz had already been in earlier in the day to find out exactly where it was otherwise they would never have found it so quickly. Howard knocked a little louder the second time when no one came.

"Who's there?" It was a man's voice and the question was asked in a very cautious manner.

"Elizabeth Harrison. You're expecting me."

They heard the bolts on the other side of the door sliding back and then the click as the locks were released. The door opened and a small, slightly bent old man in his late sixties greeted her.
"Come in. I have been expecting you," and then, peering at Howard in the darkness, he asked, "Who's this?" He sounded concerned.
"Oh it's alright," Liz assured him, "he's a friend."
"I heard about Joe," the old man said suddenly as he closed the door behind them.
"How did you know?" Howard asked. He was sure that there would not have been any publicity about his arrest.
"Soldier Andy McKern who brought me the diamonds this morning, told me."
"Brought you the diamonds?" they said together, completely taken back by his remark.
The old man noticed their expressions, asking why they seemed surprised. "Andy had said that it was lucky that he had been given the diamonds as Joe had feared that something might happen to him on his journey to Scotland, which sadly is what apparently happened. But he said that you would be coming to see me as arranged. I sent a message to Joe at the hotel last week, but as he isn't here perhaps you read my letter."
Liz looked puzzled and Howard tried to clarify the situation. "You mean that soldier had said that Elizabeth would be coming for the money that Joe should have had?" Howard asked.
"No! I gave him the money when he showed me the diamonds. He said that you knew all about it and would be coming to thank me as he was going to give you a share after he left."
"But I have Joe's diamonds here," Liz said, handing the old man the packet she took from her handbag.

Nothing was said as the old man opened the packet and tipped out the diamonds onto a black velvet cloth lying on the table. They glittered and shone in the light of a powerful lamp which the old man had switched on to examine the stones, his eye-glass pressed tightly into his right eye socket. He went quickly from one stone

to another as he examined them, his face expressionless. "Paste," he said, putting the eyeglass back on the table, "completely worthless". You might get ten pounds for them if you're lucky to be sold as costume jewellery."
Liz put her hands to her face as she took a deep breath. Howard wanted to laugh but wondered how Liz would react if he did.
The old man looked at the girl. "Where did you get them?"
Howard could see that Liz was in state of shock so he answered for her. "Joe was bringing them to Scotland with Elizabeth. She thought that they were the real ones. Do you know where this Scotsman is, by the way as we haven't seen him? He hasn't brought any money to Elizabeth." Howard tried to make it sound as if the question was quite normal in the circumstances.
The old man shrugged his shoulders, and assured them that he knew nothing of where the soldier had gone after he left his shop. "I did know him before the war as a person in the jewellery trade in Glasgow but I have no idea where he is now except that he is in the army."
Liz looked as if she was going to explode. Her face was red and her mouth open as if she was about to speak, but no words came.
"Are you sure about these diamonds? Could you not have made a mistake? Where could the fakes have come from?" Howard asked, trying to remain as calm as possible, more for Elizabeth's sake than his own.
"There's no doubt I'm afraid, no doubt at all. And in answer to your second question, I have no idea."
Howard thought that the old man appeared uncomfortable and noticed that he was giving Liz a pitiful look. "I could give you ten pounds for them," he announced suddenly.
Howard hoped that had been his first offer. "Can't you make it any more?"
The old man scratched his wrinkled chin, and looked again sympathetically at Howard's shattered companion, "Well, I suppose I could go to £12 but that's my last offer."
Liz found her voice. "Let's take it and get out of here." She sounded very angry and started to walk quickly back to the hotel.

She was at a loss to understand how it had happened and cursed Joe for his deceit.
"I'm glad he got arrested," she said without showing any feeling of remorse." He was a liar and a...a...." She couldn't find the right words and started to cry.

CHAPTER SIXTEEN

There was only one explanation in Howard's mind as to what had gone wrong. He talked to her as they hurried back to the hotel, she striding out in front.

"I've been thinking, Liz, what could have happened. I believe that Joe knew all along that the diamonds he had in his rucksack were false, in fact he must have put them there. What I don't understand is why or where he got them from, but I think that it's pretty obvious that he never intended for you to have any of the money. There was probably something that happened that he never told you about."

Liz suddenly stopped and turned round to Howard. "I remember now," she said between sobs, "Joe did go to London before Andy phoned him but he wouldn't tell me why. And we've planned all this over a lot of fake diamonds."

She stormed on, feeling not only angry, but cheated.

Howard continued to talk to her back as she strode away from him. "What I am almost certain of is that Joe had the real diamonds in his possession and the reason he got off the train at Carlisle was to hand them to his friend Andy. After he had done this and before he could get back on the train he was arrested.

"Good," Liz remarked sounding even angrier than before.

Howard had to hurry to keep up with her before continuing. "Joe's big mistake was to befriend this Andy McKern on the boat and ask him to make arrangements for the trip to Glasgow. He obviously had no idea who he was trusting with the task.

"I think it's obvious that this Scotsman knew about the dealer in Sauchiehall Street where the stones could be sold safely. He must have seen Joe arrested at Carlisle and seized the opportunity to sell the real diamonds and keep all the money for himself. Or better still, he probably told the Red Caps that Joe would be getting off the train at that station and that's why they were there, to arrest him."

Liz listened in silence to what Howard was saying as they continued to walk briskly down Renfield Street. She knew that it was too late to do anything now, whatever the explanation.
The evening seemed much colder and Howard's legs felt heavy. The journey back seemed twice as long as when they came. Liz looked as if she was going to fall over on a number of occasions but rejected Howard's offers to help each time.
They went immediately to their room at the hotel feeling very cold and dejected. The bed looked less inviting than it did earlier but perhaps in a little while when she had overcome her disappointment things might be different. Howard hoped that they could still have a wonderful night together, but saw that she was packing her case as if in a hurry, throwing her things in as quickly as she could and sobbing as she did so. Then she was gone without even saying goodbye.

As soon as Charlie was aware that Liz and Howard were clear of the premises he had bolted the door and sat down heavily on a chair and wiped the sweat from his brow with his handkerchief. At the same time Andy McKern came out of his hiding place at the back of the shop.
"You did that well Charlie, and you obviously followed Joe's instructions to the letter. Fancy him telling yer to say that I'd given the diamonds to you. Thank God they believed what you said."
Charlie had done everything that Joe had told him to do and say when he had visited him on Monday morning, but now he felt a little sorry for the girl in sending her away with a measly few pounds when the diamonds she had brought had been really worth thousands.
Charlie had not said a word about Andy being in hiding, but couldn't understand why Andy's friend, who had driven him from the Army Depot at Carlisle in a truck and had also been hiding in the back, still didn't show himself. Andy had explained that because of the damage to his arm he was unable to drive himself.

"I knew Joe had a plan but dinna ken what it was, but I see that now, it was to get rid of her and her sailor boyfriend and give 'em their just rewards - which is nothing! Oh! Clever bloody Joe."
Charlie had felt quite intimidated at the time, knowing that if he hadn't gone along with Joe's plan, he would probably get nothing himself, but he also wondered why Andy was only asking £4,000 for his part in all this when he must have known that the diamonds were worth a considerable amount more.
In spite of this Charlie began to feel a little afraid of him. He had known Andy before the war as a young apprentice in the trade and his reputation for being a little ruthless was well-known at the time, but now, no doubt due to his training as a commando, he appeared hard and his manner even more threatening. Nor did he care much for his friend who had still not shown himself since Liz and the sailor had left.
"I expect Joe will be here soon so we can all celebrate together," Charlie remarked, but was surprised at what Andy said next.
"Charlie, I don't want Joe to see me when he comes as I'm going to surprise him when you give him his £30,000, so don't breathe a word."

CHAPTER SEVENTEEN

Joe had watched Liz from a discrete distance over the weekend restraining himself not to approach her. He had then felt particularly bitter and angry when he had seen her arm in arm with Howard as soon as he arrived on Tuesday. Then again later when he saw them in the restaurant enjoying a meal together which should have been for Liz and himself. Next morning after being aware that they had spent the night together, he felt as if could murder her and was glad that he'd had the foresight to ensure that she would have nothing. Now he watched them from a discrete distance as they had their second meal and began to worry in case they were not going to the jeweller's after all. He was relieved when he saw them putting on their coats and then leaving the hotel.

Joe had followed closely behind but out of sight as Liz and Howard walked quickly from the hotel to go to Charlie MacKenzie's shop. He even began to hate Liz even more as he watched her striding out with confidence to the jeweller's where she was expecting to exchange the diamonds for the £25,000 promised in the letter she had received from Mr MacKenzie. Joe smiled to himself, thinking how he would have liked to have seen their faces when Charlie MacKenzie told them that the stones were worthless.

Joe did not have to wait very long after they had entered the jeweller's in the little side street before they came out again. Liz, obviously angry and striding out much quicker than when she had arrived there. Howard was trailing behind, trying to catch her up.

Joe chuckled quietly to himself as he hid in the shadows. It had worked. Now he was ready to collect his money. As he approached the back of the shop he wondered whether Andy had already collected his share of £4,000 What of course he did not know is that Andy was in there, and had watched Charlie carry out Joe's plan from his hiding place in the shop

By the time Joe knocked on the door Andy had gone into the other room to join his friend.

Charlie MacKenzie opened the door of his premises, greeting Joe with a huge smile.
"I've got them Joe and on the whole they are a magnificent lot. I'm extremely pleased but I couldn't help feeling sorry for the girl. You didn't tell me how pretty she was."
"She didn't look very pretty after she left here," Joe quipped, "In fact she looked positively angry." While Joe was talking he watched Charlie close the outside door and then open the safe to take out the money he had been promised. Charlie realized that Joe would not have seen the letter he had sent to the hotel reducing his offer and thought it now best to say nothing. "Here you are Joe, £30,000 and don't spend it all at once."
"When are yer expectin' Andy to come for his cut?" Joe asked out of curiosity, "or has he been already?"

There was a sudden movement behind him, which startled him.
"I'm fuckin' well here now Joe." Andy emerged from the other room and went to where the two men were standing. The atmosphere in the room did not seem quite right and Joe noticed that there was something unusual about Andy's tone of voice. This should have been a joyous occasion but Andy looked very sinister. Another soldier followed Andy out and stood next to Joe causing him to feel uncomfortable.
"Who's this son-of-a...?"
Andy interrupted Joe before he finished the question by remarking somewhat sarcastically, "I understand that certain people thought that it was you that was arrested on Carlisle station, Joe."
Joe forced a slight chuckle. "Don't talk silly, man. You know I wasn't. What's all this about?"
"But your fuckin' girl friend thinks you've been arrested," Andy said in that same mocking voice.
Joe looked hard at Andy and tried to keep calm. "But it was me that darn well told you that in the hotel". He was beginning to suspect what the Scotsman was up to and he became tense in anticipation of what might happen. He was annoyed with himself

for leaving it this late at night to come and collect his money. He should have waited until next morning.
"And, if you're in prison," Andy continued, "you winna need all that fuckin' money." He pointed in the direction of the pile of white notes.
Joe perceived a slight nod of Andy's head but before he could react, the other soldier had his hands around Joe's neck applying enormous pressure. For a second or two, Joe made an involuntary sickening sound deep in the back of his throat, his eyes and mouth opening wide. Charlie heard a crack of bone breaking and let out a stifled cry of protest. Spellbound, he watched Joe's body fall down heavily on to the floor and then lie still in a crumpled heap.
Charlie's blood drained from his face and his body began to shake. He had had no inkling of what Andy had planned to do. He felt fear as he had never experienced it before. He now realised that he was in the presence of two ruthless trained killers and began to fear for his own life. "Is he dead?" he asked, half under his breath.
"He's dead alright," Andy's friend remarked coolly, not even bending down to check. He had done this type of thing before, but previously the victims had always been the enemy.
"Right, Charlie," Andy said, calmly picking up the money that had been for Joe, "We'll get rid o' the fuckin' body and then we'll be off. Oh, and by the way, I winna tell anyone about this if I were you, or somebody may find out aboot those diamonds in your fuckin' safe! Alright?"

Charlie was still shaking uncontrollably as he stood speechless. The other soldier left the room and brought the vehicle to outside the door. He checked the street to see that no one was around before telling Andy that it was safe to bring out the body.
"Dinna worry about this chap, Charlie," Andy remarked. "Naebody will miss him - only his mither - if she's still alive." He laughed and went out of the door dragging Joe's corpse outside to the parked vehicle.

CHAPTER EIGHTEEN

Howard sat on the edge of the bed completely bewildered as to what to do next. During the last few days he had been through a fantastic experience but the tension had been exhausting. He had met a wonderful girl who had caused him more worry then he ever thought he could live through. It had been exciting having in their possession a number of, what they thought were valuable diamonds, in spite of the disappointment in the end. He did feel a pang of regret that he hadn't seen any of the money he had thought he was going to have and sorry that he wouldn't be rich after all. He then thought of Liz and wondered where she had gone. Probably back home he guessed. He couldn't get her out of his mind in spite of her leaving him as she did.
As he sat pondering all that had happened his greatest regret was that he had lost the girl he had fallen in love with. Would he ever see her again? He didn't even have her proper address. He thought at the time that she was in love with him too, but if she could just walk out without even saying goodbye then perhaps he was wrong to think that. Had she just used him after all, and now it had not worked out the way she thought it would, just left and given him no more thought?
He closed his eyes and he could see her long shining red hair covering her face when they made love and remembered what they said to each other during that glorious night, telling each other how they both felt, as they lay in each other's arms.

Returning to reality he wiped his eyes and began to think more rationally. What had he really lost? He'd lost Liz and would no doubt get over it and put it down to experience. The only other thing was the money he had expected to get from the sale of the diamonds. Then an awful thought struck him - he suddenly realised that he had a huge hotel bill to pay and had no money! Liz had kept the £12 she had received from the jeweller and although he had thought jokingly at the time to ask her for half of it he really had not had the heart to mention it again. He felt his pocket and took out what little money he had. At least he had enough to buy a couple of drinks or so. Among the coins, he saw the now worthless diamond that Liz had given him believing it to be the genuine thing at the time. It was shining almost in defiance at its minute value. It looked so real as it glistened, reflecting the lights of the room.

Howard suddenly had a hair-brained idea. Would he be able to get away with offering it to the hotel in payment of the bill in the pretence of it being real? He would be prepared to accept whatever he was offered for it, but just what value should he put on it?
First he needed to find out what the hotel bill was going to be and then he could decide. If one of the management could tell it was not a real diamond he would plead ignorance and tell them that he had been cheated by the lady who had given it to him and who they thought to have been his wife. It would be most embarrassing for him to admit that they had used the hotel for an affair, but it was the only thing that he could think of. If he left without paying the hotel already had his name, and would soon be able to trace him at the Naval Air Station at Abbotsinch, so he really had no alternative but to try something and that was the only thing he could think of. There was no other way of getting the amount of money they had spent recklessly in the belief that they would soon be rich.
When the hotel would eventually discover that the diamond was only glass and contact him he would plead innocence and borrow the money from one of his friends and pay it back later. To try to settle the bill with a counterfeit diamond was a hare-brained idea but would be fun to try.
Howard went downstairs, walked boldly to the bar, and was immediately greeted by the barman.
"Good evening, Mr Hartwell," he said cheerily, "wife not with you?"
Howard was taken a little by surprise and wondered how to answer. At least he could tell the truth to this question.

"Gone back to London I'm afraid. Could I have a half-a-pint of bitter and a chaser please?"
He hoped that the barman would not go into the matter further. Howard moved away from the bar immediately he had been served, carrying his glass of beer and his tot of scotch and sat down on his own. He began to have misgivings about what he had planned to do. Would he really be able to get away with it? Even if he did, when they discovered the truth he could be in very serious trouble, with both the Naval authorities and, no doubt, the police too!
After thinking hard about the situation he decided to tackle the problem immediately rather than wait until the next morning. If he left it till then he would not be able to sleep for thinking about what might happen. He wondered if he should still stay the night in the hotel. At least it would reduce the bill if he didn't but he still had the problem of paying the bill and how much did he actually owe? Liz had been there since Saturday!
The drink had given him courage so he went to the reception desk and told the clerk that his wife had had to go back earlier than they had planned but unfortunately, she had taken all their money with her. "Could you tell me how much we owe? I'm worried that I won't have enough with me and will have to get some when I get back to my Naval base in the morning."
"Certainly, sir. I'll find out right away."
He returned a few minutes later and gave him the bill. Howard could not believe his eyes. "Oh, that much?" was all that he was able to say.
"You will see that it includes bed for tonight and breakfast tomorrow morning for both of you," he explained.
"Oh in that case, as I will be the only one here tonight and will be leaving before breakfast, I wonder if these items could be deducted?"
"I can reduce the bill by charging for only one tonight sir but breakfast is included I'm afraid, whether you eat it or not."
It would not make much difference, Howard thought. With or without breakfast, he still had to find the money. He boldly took

the diamond from out of his pocket. "Would it be possible to try and find out how much this is worth and whether I could use it to pay the bill by any chance?" Howard tried to make his request sound as if it was quite the normal thing to have asked.
The man looked at the diamond in Howard's hand then looked very seriously at him. It was very obvious that he had never been asked before whether a hotel guest was able to pay the bill with anything other than a cheque or cash, but certainly never before with a diamond!
"I'll have to make enquiries, sir." Howard thought that he appeared to drawl out the 'sir' a bit longer than he normally did. He disappeared and was gone some time. Meanwhile, Howard was left at the desk trying not to imagine the sort of conversation that was going on behind closed doors.

After what appeared to be an interminable length of time the clerk emerged with the manager of the hotel close behind him. Howard's heart began to beat a little faster
"I understand that you are making enquiries as to whether you can pay you bill with a diamond. Is that right, sir?"
"Well, nearly right. You see my wife..."
"Yes, yes," the manager interrupted, "I fully understand the situation you find yourself in. The desk clerk has explained everything to me. I may be able to help you. Fortunately we have staying in the hotel this evening a Mr Campbell, who is a jeweller, and whom I have already contacted. He will be down in a moment to value your diamond. If you would take a seat in the lounge I will bring him to you when he arrives."

CHAPTER NINETEEN

Howard's heart sank. 'An expert in diamonds' he had said! One glance and he would tell him what he already knew. He wondered whether he should leave now and hope that they would not bother to try and find him. Howard heard voices and he stood up to greet the diamond expert. He was a man in his middle-fifties, short and stocky, not as tall as Howard and much overweight for his age but looking extremely prosperous in his dark grey tweed suit. Howard did not feel relaxed in spite of his warm smile and firm handshake.

"Please sit down, Mr er.."

"Hartwell," Howard said. Obviously the manager had not told him his name, or was this the man's way he always greeting his clients.

"I understand that you have a diamond requiring a value. Can I see it?"

Howard gave him the diamond and even before he produced his eyeglass and put it to his eye, Howard expected him to say, "Glass!"

He examined it carefully but not for long. "Where did you get this Mr Hartwell?"

"It was given to me as a present," Howard told him truthfully.

"You have a very fine stone here," he said. "I would quickly estimate it to be worth over five hundred pounds."

Howard could not believe his ears. "How much did you say?" he asked, trying not to sound too surprised.

"I could be wrong," the jeweller admitted, "It could be a lot more. I'd need to examine it more carefully in better light and at length and find out the number of carats."

Howard tried to remain calm although he was sure that the man must have heard his heart beating hard against the wall of his chest. If only Liz was here, he thought, but he remembered that she also had one that she had taken from out of the envelope. Was her diamond the same or was this an odd one that had been mixed up with the others? Perhaps they had all been genuine diamonds and that man MacKenzie had tricked them both He put all this out

of his mind for the moment. The important thing was to sell the diamond before this fellow changed his mind.
"How much will you give me for it?" Howard asked. "I need to sell it urgently."
"Don't be in such a hurry young man. You want to get the best price for it and I'll try to do that if that is what you would like me to do."
Howard didn't want to wait that long. Even if this man had said it was worth more than he had originally valued he would be satisfied with five hundred pounds. "I need to get back to the camp first thing in the morning. Why can't you give me something for it now? I need the money urgently."
"How can I be sure that it is yours to sell?" the man asked calmly. "How do I know that you haven't stolen it, or, whoever gave it to you didn't steal it? Forgive me for saying so but it seems strange that someone should give you such a valuable diamond and then you be prepared to accept less than its real value."
Howard hadn't expected to be questioned so closely and he could almost see the police coming into the hotel to question him even more thoroughly. He began to wish that he had left it until the morning, taken it into one of the jeweller's shops in Glasgow and then accepted what he would be offered for it. Some of them would be only too pleased to get a bargain. But of course he hadn't known its worth until now. He thought that he could still do that tomorrow, but as he had to be back on the Station before eight o'clock and the shops would not be open until after nine, he would have to come back in the evening. No, he needed to sell it now if he could. He decided to take a bold and more positive approach.
"If you don't want it, I'll sell it tomorrow for what I can get for it, and I'll just pay you the fee for valuing it for me," Howard told him. He noticed that Mr Campbell suddenly looked a little disappointed.
"I didn't say that I didn't want it," he replied quickly. "Give me a little time to examine it more closely and I'll make you an offer provided that you sign a guarantee that it is yours to sell."
"I'll do that willingly," Howard said.

He wondered whether the diamond that Liz had was also real. If she too discovered that it was and contacted him to find out about whether his was valuable too there would be no one else she could tell so he could sign without fear of anyone finding out where the diamond had come from. After all, Joe was the real thief, and he had been arrested, although perhaps not for the theft of diamonds. If all the diamonds had been real, he and Liz had been deliberately cheated out of the money, but why? Knowing that Joe had stolen the diamonds by murdering a Belgian jeweller there was no way that he was going to try and find out. His first concern was to get rid of the one that he had and now the opportunity had just arrived.

The jeweller had moved to a small table with a bright table lamp and returned after thoroughly examining the stone.

"I'll give you five hundred and fifty pounds for it," he said firmly immediately after he had sat down and kept the diamond in his hand apparently reluctant to hand it back.

Howard was impressed at the way that the jeweller had stated the figure he was prepared to give. There was no mistaking that it was a 'take it or leave it' offer and no doubt it was the way that this fellow always conducted his negotiations in his business deals. There would be no point in haggling. Howard made his decision accepting his offer after only brief pause. Mr Campbell produced a printed form from his inside pocket and called the Manager over to witness Howard's signature. Howard could see at a glance that it was an official document drawn up to ensure that Mr Campbell, or his company, would be in the clear should any of his purchases prove to be stolen goods. Mr Campbell wrote out the cheque, they shook hands, and the jeweller left the room. With the agreement of the Manager of the hotel, Howard endorsed the cheque, paid his hotel bill and pocketed the substantial balance.

Later that evening, after spending over three shillings in the bar, Howard found it difficult to sleep for thinking about the soldier whom Joe had befriended and trusted. Now that he had found that the diamond Liz had given him was real his earlier theory of what had happened at Carlisle was certainly wrong. The diamonds they took to the jeweller must been the real ones after all and the costume jewellery had never existed. They were in his rucksack all the time. Because Andy had seen Joe arrested he probably thought that it was his chance to have all the money.

It would be easy to get Mr MacKenzie to lie, the man who Andy must have known before the war, and they would be together in the deceit so when he and Liz took the diamonds to the jeweller he told them that they were false.

But nothing mattered now except for one thing. How could he contact Liz?

He began to feel sorry for her. She had been devastated after being told that the stones were not genuine, and he wondered whether she really had gone home after she stormed out of the hotel.

CHAPTER TWENTY

Elizabeth Harrison had arrived at the Central Station just in time to board the overnight express to London. There was nothing else she could have done but to go back home with only the money that the jeweller had given her, some of which she had used to buy her ticket.

She sat in a corner seat by the window of an empty compartment and began to cry. She had set out with Joe less than a week ago with such high hopes of becoming rich, but so much had changed since that time. Firstly, Joe had been arrested and there was no way of knowing what had happened to him.

Secondly, the diamonds he had been carrying had proved to be worthless and thirdly she had let down the only really decent man she had ever met in her life by promising him half of the fortune she had hoped to make, only for him to finish with nothing. Indeed, she had left him to pay a huge hotel bill, which she knew he would not be able to afford. It saddened her to think that he did not deserve that sort of treatment. She had cajoled him into helping her and he had managed to get the diamonds off the train safely, agreeing with her demands all along the way. Even when they discovered that the diamonds were not real he had not grumbled, although he must have been disappointed that he got nothing out of it after doing everything she had asked him to do. It was true that she had let him make love to her but to leave him as she did was unforgivable

Thinking about Howard made her cry even more. She thought at one time that she had fallen in love with him and he had told her that he loved her, but the traumatic events that followed were dominant in her mind and all she could think of was getting away from Glasgow.

As she sat quietly on the train with her thoughts all the tension of the last few days gradually began to fade away, but the disappointment of returning home with nothing left her feeling dejected. She was tired and weak from all her crying, and this, together with the effect of the rhythm of the train on the rails, lulled her off to sleep.

She awoke with a jerk as the train pulled into a station. It had reached Carlisle and she found herself staring at the almost empty platform with an uncontrollable urge to try and find out what had really happened to Joe and if he had been arrested for any other reason than just being a deserter. She was right to not want him to get off the train at the time, especially as they both knew that it might have been very risky to do so.
Carrying her case she paraded up and down that same platform wondering if there might be someone she could ask at this time of night who could remember the incident and be able to give her some information. If they had found out that he was a murderer she knew that she would never ever hear from him again. A porter saw her looking around and asked if he could help. Liz thought that there would be no harm in asking him a question or two.
"There was an American soldier who was arrested here last Friday," she said. "I was on the same train going to Scotland and I wondered whether you knew why he had been arrested and what had happened to him."
The porter looked at her very seriously. "Did you know him, madam?" he asked.
Liz thought that she had to be careful how the answer that question and hesitated for a few seconds. The porter remained looking at her, too intently she thought. "Well, I think he was the same American who I travelled with in the same compartment from London. He said he was going to Glasgow but he got off the train here for some reason and didn't return. He seemed such a nice person and there was such a commotion on the platform when he was arrested. I was only enquiring out of curiosity."
"Are you getting back on the train madam?" the porter asked. "It'll be leaving very shortly if that is what you intend to do."
"I was wondering what time the next train to London is due as I would like to stay here for a little while longer," Liz said, trying to sound very calm and in full control of herself.

"The London train from Edinburgh will be arriving in about three-quarters of an hour an hour," the porter informed her in his official voice. "You'll be able to catch that one," and then surprised her by adding, "Still worried about that soldier are you madam?"
"Well, I would like to know - purely out of curiosity of course," Liz said again.
"Of course madam. I'll go and make some enquiries for you, meanwhile why don't you go the waiting room. It'll be warmer in there." He walked very briskly away towards the Station Master's Office.
Liz was beginning to wonder whether perhaps she should not have sounded so interested in what had happened to Joe and get back on the train, but it was too late! She heard the whistle blowing while she had been talking to the porter and, at that moment, she saw the train beginning to leave.

She sat down on one of the wooden benches inside the very poorly lit waiting room all alone wondering if she had done the right thing. The porter was a long time, and she was beginning to feel very cold. She heard the door opening behind her and turned to see two policemen coming in her direction. It was the middle of the night and Liz thought it strange that two policemen had come to see her at this hour.
"Are you the lady that was asking about the American soldier who was arrested here last week?" the taller one asked politely. "I understand that you knew him."
"Well..er..no. Not really knew him," Liz answered tentatively.
"We have reason to believe that you did." He now spoke with more authority in his voice and then added without waiting for Liz to reply, "I wonder whether you'd mind coming with us to the station we would like to ask you some questions."
No one spoke as she sat alone in the back seat of the police car on the way to the police station. Although she was worried the journey gave her time to think. She wondered what she should admit to and whether she should explain her relationship with Joe. What did they know about him? The authorities must have found

out that he was a deserter but did they know about the diamonds? What was more important, had they found out that he had murdered that Belgian civilian? They arrived at the police station much too quickly for her to be clear in her mind what she should say.
She was taken to a small room and sat facing a desk. Two plain-clothes detectives came in and sat down facing her on the opposite side.
"First, would you tell us who you are?" said the older of the two men, "and where you've been?"
Liz gave them her full name and address, and told the men that she had travelled to Scotland with her boy friend who was in the Navy. She said that they had spent only one night together in the Renfield Hotel as a married couple and was now returning home.
The one night was the only time he could get leave. If they wanted to check on her story they would find the last part to be true as the people at the hotel in Glasgow had no knowledge of Joe, and she knew that the room had been originally booked in her name of Harrison. She felt satisfied that she had covered her tracks so far.
"Then why are you so interested in the soldier who was arrested on the station here in Carlisle?" the younger detective asked.
This was the question she had been dreading. She hesitated before answering, trying to find an answer which would sound plausible. Just to say that she was curious had not convinced the porter and she knew the police would receive it with scepticism.
But before she could answer the older man reached into a folder, which was open in front of him, took out a photograph and slid it across to her. "How long have you known this man?" he asked seriously.
Her eyes opened wide as she looked first at the photograph of the G.I. and then at the two detectives. "I've never seen this man before in my life," she answered truthfully. "Was this the man who was arrested?"
The older man leaned forward to look at Liz more closely. "Do you expect us to believe that you have never ever seen this man before?"

"You can believe what you like," Liz replied, now feeling more confident and relieved that it wasn't Joe that had been taken away by the Military Police. She was now anxious to clear up this confusion very quickly as she wanted her mind to be clear and try to discover what had really happened to Joe. At the same time she didn't want them to know that she knew him in case they later discovered who he really was and what he'd done, so she explained to them that a G.I. who had been travelling in the same compartment as Howard and she had introduced himself to them as Joe Peabody and had got off the train at Carlisle. She told them that he had said that he would be back but he never got back on the train as far as she knew, unless he had got on that part of the train that went to Edinburgh.
"But when we saw the American soldier being taken away, we assumed that it was this fellow we had met," Liz explained, "And now, on my way back to London, I was curious to know the reason why he was arrested. He seemed such a nice person. But this isn't him," she repeated, pointing to the photograph. "So it doesn't matter."
"So it was only curiosity that made you break your journey," the detectives remarked. "This Joe Peabody, did he not have a case with him or any other luggage?"
Liz had told one lie and now she was about to tell another. If she gave them the right answer, she hoped that they wouldn't ask her any more questions. "No, I don't really remember. I didn't take that much notice, unless he was carrying a small rucksack, but my attention was on the arrest and now I can see that it wasn't him."
The detectives looked puzzled. "Strange that he didn't return after telling you that he'd be back. And he didn't leave anything on the train?"
She had to be careful how she answered, because she had thrown away the small rucksack that had originally contained the diamonds and Joe's things and now she began to worry that it might have been found and that the police were searching for the owner. "Well, I really didn't take much notice, but there was

nothing left belonging to him on the train when he didn't return. What he had he must have taken with him."
They asked a few more questions about Joe which she pretended not to know the answers to, repeating that they had only met on the train, and the detectives appeared finally convinced that Liz was telling the truth.
"Perhaps you would give me the name of this boy-friend of yours as we might want to confirm your story: purely routine, you understand."
"Of course," Liz replied, and, after giving them what they wanted asked, "Can I go now and catch the train to London? I hope I haven't missed it." She looked up at the clock and wondered whether she would be able to get back to the station in time.
One of the men looked at his wrist-watch. "No! You have plenty of time. My sergeant will run you back, Miss," said the older of the two men, "and thank you for your co-operation in this matter. If we need you again we have your address but I doubt if that will be necessary."

On the way to the station she quizzed the detective as to the identity of the American soldier who had been arrested and why. He told her that he had been wanted for murdering a couple of black American soldiers and that the Military Police had seen him board the Glasgow train at Euston. They were at every stop waiting for him to get off as they were reluctant to arrest him on the train knowing that he carried a gun. "When he left the train here in Carlisle he was arrested immediately and taken away. He'll be tried for murder. We thought you might have been involved when you began to make enquiries. I believe the American Police searched the trains believing that he had an accomplice but found no one, but now we wonder if the G.I. who left your compartment was the other man we were looking for and didn't return because he saw his friend arrested."
Liz had asked the question but was only half listening to his explanation, knowing that they had drawn the wrong conclusions about Joe but she was trying to work out why he had not returned

after getting off the train as planned and why hadn't he turned up at the hotel? And what of the diamonds? Had he known that they were fakes? Is that why he had not contacted her in Glasgow? Had he seen her with Howard? Perhaps they were real after all and he had been confident that she would take them to that jeweller in Sauchiehall Street who would pretend that they were fakes so that Joe could have all the money? That couldn't be true though either. The jeweller wouldn't be that dishonest surely. There must have been a switch. Was the Scottish soldier all part of the plan? She felt that she had been used but the only good thing that had come out of it was that she had met Howard and now could not stop thinking about him.

Thanking the driver as she got out of the car the thought occurred to her that perhaps she was never intended to have half of the money. Was this was the real reason that Joe didn't turn up and getting off the train at Carlisle was part of his plan It all seemed too risky for Joe to have relied on Liz doing exactly what he wanted her to, with the real diamonds, but it did not make sense to go to all that trouble if they were fakes. If Joe didn't want her to have some of the money he need not have promised her any of it or even bothered take her to Glasgow. She concluded that perhaps the diamonds had been real after all and that soldier McKern must have robbed Joe, but if that was the case, why hadn't Joe contacted her and had something happened to him? Perhaps she would never find out.

Liz could never have imagined that less than two weeks later he would be found in the river Clyde murdered.

Liz sat quietly in the train as it sped towards London. She felt in her bag and took out the large diamond she had been told was worthless. She was still feeling hurt that she had lost all that money that she had hoped would make her rich. Suddenly she felt very lonely. Surely Howard would never want to see her again after the way she had treated him. She should never have deserted him like that. She began to miss him dreadfully and longed to see him again. Perhaps she should write to him and say that she was

CHAPTER TWENTY-ONE

During the following week after returning to "The Cricketer's Arms" Liz had tried to forget all about what might had happened to Joe, but when she had learned that it was not he that had been arrested, or that they were not carrying the real diamonds it now seemed obvious to her that she had been used and that there had never been any intention of her receiving any of the money. That was why she had not been surprised that she hadn't seen or even heard from him since she was back home. But now in discovering that he had been murdered perhaps those early conclusions had been wrong. She contemplated that perhaps Joe had been killed by that man called McKern. After all Mr MacKenzie had told them that it was he who had taken the real diamonds to him. If Joe had been alive why didn't he take them? The whole thing seemed clear to her and she hoped that the real murderer would be discovered.
The customers were surprised to see Liz so quiet that evening and although she went to bed late as usual she could not sleep. She was convinced that the police would arrive early the next morning to question her and would discover that she had really known this American who had been murdered whom she told them was Joe Peabody.

Now she was wide-awake thinking about Howard. He had been in her thoughts constantly ever since she had left Scotland and she hoped that he had forgiven her for running away. She longed to see him again but it was a long way to go just to say that she was sorry and he might have even refused to see her. The one night they had spent together had been the happiest of her life and had also been a turning point from the sort of life she had led previously. But now, because of what had happened to Joe, she knew that it was imperative that she saw him and felt excited at the prospect in spite of the seriousness of the situation.
She would have to go to Paisley as soon as possible but what excuse could she make to her employer? She suddenly had an idea and hoped it would work.

She was up very early and met the postman as she had planned during the night, then came back into the pub and put the letters on the table in the kitchen. She found some notepaper under the bar counter and went to her room to write a letter to herself. When Cornelius came into the kitchen she appeared to be very upset and she was holding a letter in her hand.
"I had a letter from my Aunt in Glasgow this morning," she lied. "She's very ill and wondered whether I could possibly go and see her."
The landlord of the pub looked at her in disbelief. "You mean that you really do have an aunt in Glasgow, as well as the one here in the village?"
"Edith Harrison, here in the village, is my father's sister - she never married and I really do have another aunt in Glasgow," she lied again. "She's my mother's widowed sister. You remember I told you that I visited her recently but she said nothing about being ill. She came down to London for the funeral when my mother and father were killed in that air-raid and she told me then that I was her only relative...I really ought to go."
Cornelius Hill was not fully convinced that she was telling the truth. Liz had only mentioned her aunt in Glasgow when she had used her as an excuse when she went to Scotland with Joe only a few weeks ago. He had never thought that she existed, but now, she appeared to be really concerned about her sick aunt. In spite of that something did not seem quite right to him.
"Can I see?" he asked, reaching out for the piece of paper she was holding. He looked carefully at the almost indecipherable scrawl written on it, but it looked genuine enough, with an address in Glasgow at the top and dated three days previously. Liz had made a good job of it.
Cornelius turned the letter over, "No envelope?"
"Of course there was. I didn't bring it down. Can I go today Neil?"
"If you must you must." Then he waved his hand in resignation, "Yes, of course. You'd better go straight away."

Cornelius searched for a while after Liz had left as he thought that he recognised the type of paper used in the letter purported to have been received from her aunt. He soon found the writing pad his barmaid had used to write what he now knew to be a fictitious letter. It confirmed his suspicion that there was no aunt in Glasgow and she must have had an ulterior motive for wanting to go so quickly after learning of Joe's death He wondered how deeply she had been involved in his murder.
Something had been worrying her ever since she had returned from Scotland, and a couple of times he had caught her in tears. Once he had joked by telling her that he thought she was in love and that had caused a real outburst. He had never questioned her as to why Joe had not come back, assuming that he had rejoined his unit. When customers had asked her where her good-looking American was, she had quickly changed the subject. He wondered whom she was really going to see in Scotland but decided that if anyone asked him where she was, he would tell them that she had gone to visit her sick aunt in Glasgow as she had told him.
Early the following morning two plain-clothes policemen arrived at "The Cricketer's Arms," and asked if they could have a few words with Elizabeth Harrison.

Liz slept in fits and starts on the train most of the way to Glasgow. However at Carlisle she awoke with a start, as if an alarm had gone off in her head. She stared out of the carriage window. The evening light cast shadows across the platform, which gave the place a strange but peaceful look and in complete contrast to when she and Howard had last looked out of the window at the dimly-lit station the last time. She wondered whether Howard had thought any more about her since that time. As the train began to move again she could see in her mind's eye the American being led away by the Military Police, a man whom they both thought at the time to have been Joe.
Liz realised that Howard might not have learnt that it was another American that had been arrested on the platform at Carlisle railway station. He had told her previously that hardly anyone on

CHAPTER TWENTY-TWO

Howard lay on his bed wondering why he had not heard from Liz following a visit from the police over a week ago. He had been scared when he was told that two plain clothed officers were waiting in the Padre's office to question him believing that they had probably learnt about the diamonds from Joe. They first asked him to confirm whether it was he who had travelled to Glasgow with his girl friend, Elizabeth Harrison, and then said that did he agree that they thought they had seen the American soldier who had been in their same carriage, arrested on Carlisle station.
He had immediately wondered how they had found that out but had been confused when they had said, 'thought they had seen'. What had they meant by that? Of course they had seen Joe arrested?
Then before he could ask a question, they had surprised him by saying, "You may like to know, that it wasn't your American companion who you both saw taken away, but another American soldier."
When he had asked how they knew all this they had told him what had happened when Elizabeth had got off the train at Carlisle on her way back to London.
He still waited for them to ask about Joe, "So why question me? he had asked.
They had said that it was just routine and just needed him to confirm that he was the girl's boyfriend and that the American had just been travelling with them both in the same compartment until he got out at Carlisle.
"But why the interest our American?" he had asked trying to sound as though his question was of just out of curiosity.
They had said that the police at Carlisle thought that their American might have been an accomplice of the other one who had been arrested but now they didn't think so.
He had breathed a sigh of relief, thankful that it appeared to be the only thing they wanted to know.

The police had then departed with the remarks, "Don't worry, sir, we only asked for you to confirm the girl's story."

Howard had quickly realised that when Liz found out that it hadn't been Joe who had been arrested, she had probably told the Carlisle police nothing else, but he now couldn't understand why they hadn't seen Joe at the hotel and wondered why.
In view of this revelation of what had happened at Carlisle he thought the fact that Joe was free must be worrying Liz so it seemed strange that she had not contacted him. Perhaps he had got it all wrong and Joe had been to see her and that was why she had not contacted him. At least he had got something for all his trouble.
Just when he thought that it would be best to forget the whole affair he had a message to say that the police were here again to see him. This time it was a police sergeant and another police officer and Howard assumed that they now knew more about Joe than they did the last time the police came to question him.
He wondered how he would answer them but then taken aback when they told him that the body of the American soldier whom they had travelled with, had been found in the Clyde, murdered.
"Apparently," said the sergeant, "he had been put in the river at about the same time that Miss Harrison was interviewed by the police in Carlisle, but not particularly because of that, we would like to have a word with her again"
"Why? We never saw the American again. The fact that she stopped at Carlisle to ask about him proves that."
"I agree that it seems unlikely," the inspector explained to him, "that she had anything to do with his murder, but we would still like to speak to her again because she didn't tell the police the truth. You see when the local police called at the pub where she worked they found that she had left the previous day. The landlord had apparently told them that she had said that she was going to Glasgow to visit her sick aunt but had seemed very upset when she read about the American being murdered. He also told them that he thought that she knew this American and had heard his

name mentioned a time or two but apparently he'd never heard of you. "So how come she's your girlfriend?"
The sudden question took Howard by surprise and he hesitated before answering. Howard guessed that she had told her employer that story about visiting her aunt as an excuse and that he was sure that she was now coming to see him. But how should he answer the question that was asked. He considered that they would find out sooner or later so he thought that he might as well tell them the truth.
"Alright we met on the train and had a couple of day's together in a hotel."
The two policeman looked at each other and were temporary speechless. The sergeant eventually found his voice. "Well we wondered whether she might try to contact you here so, if, or when she does, perhaps you would let us know when she turns up."

Howard was glad to see them go. Ever since the first time the police came to question him, he was not able to get what had happened out of his mind. It was not only been the belief at the time that Joe had been arrested, or why he seemed to have disappeared, or the disappointment about the diamonds and the loss of the money, but it had been Liz herself who had dominated his thoughts.
Now, after their second visit, he lay there thinking what might have happened since that day when Liz left him in that hotel. Had she been able to find out where Joe had been after he left the train and why he was murdered and dumped in the Clyde? The police had told him that he had been in the water for almost a couple of weeks. Now, apparently, they couldn't find Liz. Where was she? No doubt as they said, on the train heading for Paisley with the intention of coming to see him. If it were true, and he guessed that it was, he became quite excited at the prospect. He wondered whether they would find her before she came to him and then he realised that they would probably be unable to recognise her and wait until she arrived.

Although they had spent so little time together her departure had left a strange emptiness in his life. He had often thought about writing to her to arrange a meeting but the manner of her leaving had prevented him from putting pen to paper.

Meanwhile, Liz could not wait to see him and hoped that he had not been moved away. It crossed her mind that perhaps she ought to have written to him first, but she had been anxious to get away quickly in case the police came to the pub to question her. She realised that others could have been to see Howard already to check her story. The police at Carlisle did ask her where he was stationed and she hoped that he had managed to convince them that he knew nothing about Joe except that she had travelled with him in the same compartment. If they had been to see Howard he would now know that it hadn't been Joe that they had seen arrested, but wondered if he also knew that he'd been murdered
She also worried about having left him to sort out the hotel bill and wondered how badly he had taken that. She hoped that he had not retaliated by telling the police about the faked diamonds, especially the one she had given him.
If only the train would hurry, but as usual, the train was late getting in and by the time she had grabbed a sandwich and a cup of tea on Glasgow's Central Station and had caught a tram to Paisley, she realised that it was far too late to go to see Howard so would wait until the next day.
She found a small hotel in the square and booked in for two nights knowing that she wouldn't get back to London until the day after tomorrow. She told them that she was going to visit her husband who was in the Navy and thought perhaps that he might be able to join her later.
Next day she thought that it would be better if she went about lunchtime to see Howard and set off to walk the mile or so to the Royal Naval Air Station. At the entrance was a large sign with the words "HMS Sanderling" emblazoned on it. She asked the white-gaitered guard at the gate if it was possible to see Air Mechanic Howard Hartwell, as it was very urgent.

"Urgent is it?" the guard asked in his broad Wales accent. "You'll be his second visitor this morning now. He's already had two plain-clothes policemen to see him. He must be very important but probably not a criminal, as they didn't take him away, see. Who shall I say wants to see him and what for? I have to be very careful now. You might be a spy. - Mind you, a very pretty one."
Liz felt the blood rushing to her cheeks. It took a lot to make her blush, but very few girls apart from the W.R.N.S came to the gatehouse, and this handsome Welshman was enjoying flirting with a civilian girl. It was obviously true what they said about sailors she decided. His manner reminded her of Howard. She had hoped that her reason for wanting to see him would sound convincing.
"I've come for the same reason as the police and all the way from Dorset in England. Please, it's very important that I see him."
"Well, the police have only just left. It's a wonder that you didn't see their car. It's nearly time for the mid-day meal so we should catch him before he goes back to the hangars on the other side of the airfield."
He flicked a switch and spoke into a microphone. Loudspeakers throughout the camp boomed out the message. "D'yer hear there. D'yer hear there. Would Air Mechanic Howard Hartwell report to the main gate immediately? This message is urgent."
When the announcement came over the Tannoy that Howard was to report to the gatehouse it was not as much of a shock as it might have been if the police had not already spoken to him about their assumption that Liz might come to see him. He suspected that the call for him to report at the gatehouse was because she had arrived and therefore he was not surprised to see her.

They stood looking at each other for a few seconds neither knowing what to say and then Liz moved forward and gave him a kiss in greeting. Howard smiled and gave her a hug in return. He thought she looked older and her face was a peculiar shade of pinkish grey. They moved away from the watching guard before

he spoke. There was no need for him to ask why she was there, or for her to explain.
"So it wasn't Joe who we saw arrested after all and now he's been murdered!"
Liz didn't look surprised. "The guard has just told me that the police have been, so I suppose they've told you, but what have you told them?" She now wanted to know the answer quickly.
"They've been to see me twice but they're quite concerned that they haven't been able to find you and told me to contact them when you arrive."
Without waiting for her reaction he asked, "When you found out that it wasn't Joe we saw taken away why didn't you let me know? I had to guess that you went to see the police at Carlisle but wasn't that a risky thing to do? And more importantly, as it wasn't Joe that we saw arrested, why didn't he come and look for us at the hotel? Have you any idea who might have murdered him and when?"
Liz didn't know which question to answer first but quickly told him what happened at Carlisle. "Do you think I haven't thought about those questions a lot, but I'm sorry that I didn't write to you to tell you and that you had to find out from the police."
"But do you realise Liz, that after speaking to your pub boss, the police also are certain that you knew Joe and have guessed that you are coming here to see me! We're getting ourselves into an awful mess if we're not careful."
Liz grabbed his hand. "You're not going to let them know I'm here, are you? I'm sure that no one has seen me. I came last night and stayed at a small hotel in Moss Street booking in there for a couple of nights so stop worrying. As far as what I told the police at Carlisle, I've already thought about that, and ready to admit that I've not been truthful. I'll say that I was ashamed to tell them that Joe and I were going to have a few days together in Glasgow but when I thought he'd been arrested, you took his place."
"Good God! What will the police think about you - and about me for that matter?"

"It is something we'll have to say to take away any suspicion the police may have about us. You haven't told them anything that could lead the police to suspect that we had been involved in any way with Joe's death, have you?"
"No! of course not, because we haven't, and nothing was mentioned about diamonds either because I don't think they know. By the way Liz, how much did you get for your diamond?"
"What diamond?"
"The ones that you took out of the packet at the hotel before we took them to that lying jeweller. You do realise now that they were ALL real and we were swindled."
Liz's eyes opened wide in disbelief, "What do you mean, 'real'? I threw mine away after that jeweller had told us that they were all fakes."
"Fakes? I got five hundred and fifty pounds for mine from a jeweller I met at the hotel. Even then I know I was paid less than it was worth!"
"Oh! Are you telling me that mine was real too?"
"Pretty certain."
Liz covered her blushes with her hands and told him how sorry she was about leaving him like she did and of throwing her diamond away.
"We can't worry about that now." He took hold of her hand as he spoke and she made no attempt to stop him.
"What have you done with all that money?"
"The hotel manager cashed the cheque for me to pay the bill and I put the rest into a bank account."
"But why did the jeweller lie to us? What do you think happened?
He explained that he thought he had solved the mystery of what went on and who had been involved in swindling them and was pretty certain that it was the Scottish soldier and the jeweller together.
"I have thought about it many times," he told her, "but can find no other explanation. What I am certain of is that they were too clever for us, but at least we did get something out of it, or at least I did."

As she listened her face began returning to its natural colour and her eyes looked a lot more kindly than before.
"I'm sorry I left you to pay the hotel bill Howard, but I've brought enough money with me to pay back what it cost you."
"There's no need for that, Liz. Remember I told you how much I got for the diamond from a jeweller in the hotel and that..." Howard stopped in mid sentence. "Oh my god! I've just realised that if they find out where we stayed in Glasgow the Hotel Manager will remember me - he arranged the sale. There can't be many people in Naval uniform who pay their hotel bill with a diamond! And when they question me about that it will be difficult to hide from the truth and my diamond won't fit in with any part of our story. And how will we be able to explain about that friend of Joe's who booked the room?. Oh heavens! It's a real hornet's nest." Howard's brain was beginning to work overtime.
"Look, Liz, the people here know here that the police have been to question me so it should be fairly easy for me to get a couple of days compassionate leave to try and sort things out. I'll meet you as soon as possible in that cafe in the high street."
The guard watched her go, never taking his eyes off her shapely legs, until she disappeared round a bend in the road.

CHAPTER TWENTY-THREE

Liz waited impatiently until Howard arrived at the cafe. It seemed a lifetime since he had passed the diamonds over the table to her. She had chosen to sit in the same seats that they had sat in the last time they were here and the same red-haired girl who had served them then took their order. Howard looked across the table into Elizabeth's beautiful green eyes recalling the conversation they had had there previously. He remembered how she had teased him by offering him a bonus if he went with her back to the hotel. That had excited him and he was aware of that same feeling now. Grinning broadly, he asked facetiously, "Are you going to offer me the same as you did the last time we were here?" She didn't respond with a smile as he expected but had a look in her eyes he had not seen before.

"I hope," she began in almost a whisper, "no, I mean, I wish..." She looked at Howard, unable to continue, suddenly realising how much she loved this man sitting opposite her. It was a sort of love that she had not experienced before, but now he was teasing her about what had happened the last time they were here and she felt ashamed about the way she had acted then.

Howard noticed that her hands were shaking a little as they rested on the table. He took them gently into his. They felt soft, almost without life. It was not hard to see what Liz was trying to say and the look in her eyes told him what he wanted to know. Leaning forward he said quietly, "Liz, I've missed you so and I do love you. I've thought of you all the time since you went away. I can't believe you're here."

She wanted to tell him that she loved him too, but if she spoke now she knew that she would burst into tears like a schoolgirl. A tear trickled down her cheek and Howard knew that there was no need for her to say anything. He handed her his handkerchief and told her to dry her eyes.

"Why are we being so unhappy?" Howard said, giving her a smile. She smiled back and now able to speak, told him that she was in love with him and how much she had missed him. "I feel better

now that you're here. I didn't know what to do when I saw Joe's photograph in the newspaper."
He bent down and kissed her hands and ran his hands over her smooth fingers. "And where is your wedding ring young lady? Don’t tell me that you have divorced me already."
"Oh Howard, I threw it out of the train window together with the diamond!"
She paused for a moment or two realising what she had done and then they both laughed at how ridiculous it all was. He reached over the table and kissed her. "Look, we'll do nothing for the moment. I just want to sit here with you and forget all what has happened before," and then he added quickly, "well, perhaps not everything."
"But we can't just do nothing, Howard. We will have to go to the police sometime and explain what we know. They probably suspect us as being involved with Joe's murder. What are we to do?"
Howard felt that he had to take hold of the situation as Liz appeared to be unable to think clearly. "Well, my sweet, I think we had better go to your hotel in Moss Street and explain that I am your fiancé and see if they have a room for me to stay there."
Liz dropped her gaze and looked somewhat coy, "Oh dear, I told them that you were my husband and that you may be able to join me later."
Howard grinned, "I seem to have been down this road before! Caught out like the last time and again without any night gear."
Now it was Elizabeth's turn to smile. "I told Neil that I was just going on a brief visit to my imaginary Aunt who was ill, so I also have very little with me. I never even thought of a nightie!"
"If I'm joining you that's the last thing you'll need tonight young lady," Howard chuckled.
They left the cafe and noticed for the first time that the sun was shining and that it was a glorious spring evening. They arrived at the hotel, and with her appetite returned, Liz suddenly announced that apart from a few sandwiches, she had had very little to eat since she had left the village the day before. Howard hadn't eaten

any lunch either so they sat in the restaurant of the small hotel to enjoy a leisurely meal together.
"We have very little to worry about really," Howard said, trying to reassure her and taking hold of her hands across the table. "We haven't murdered anybody, stolen anything, or committed any crime as far as I can see. And we aren't the first couple in the world to have a few days in a hotel pretending to be married. I don't think it's a serious crime doing that." Then adding, as he squeezed her hands, "And, what's more we are going to commit the same crime tonight."
Liz liked what he was doing but her thoughts were elsewhere for the moment. "But what about your diamond?" she asked, still sounding worried in spite of Howard's confidence that everything would be alright. "There are a lot of people at that hotel in Glasgow who will remember us."
"I've had second thoughts about that. There's only that diamond that I sold in the hotel to worry about and I'll have to think of something to explain that. There's no reason at all, as far as I can see, that the police will be able to find out about the rest of the diamonds, or that they even existed. Think about it Liz. The only people who knew we had them were Joe who is dead, the jeweller and that Scottish soldier who supposedly brought the real ones to him earlier. The last two are bound to keep quiet and the first one has no option."
Elizabeth noticed that he was being a little flippant but ignored his remark. as she felt sorry for what had happened to Joe.
Howard had often thought about that soldier and what part he had played to do them out of the money.
"I think that I've just solved it Liz," he said slowly and deliberately. "After Joe had met that soldier Andy McKern, he either prevented him from getting back on the train or saw that it was impossible to do so with so many police about. He then later murdered him. He would have known that you had the diamonds and, after making sure that you were in the hotel, he assumed that you would take them to the jeweller as planned. He would have to wait until we had taken the diamonds to him of course, which we

did, and if we didn't he would have tried to get them off you. It was easier for him to get that fellow MacKenzie to cooperate. Joe never made it because he was already dead."
"And that's where your theory goes wrong my darling amateur detective," Liz said a friendly mocking way. "I think you have assumed too many things. Firstly, McKern had never seen me and secondly, my name was crossed out in the hotel register. He didn't know your name and unless Joe had told him he knew nothing about you, so I don't believe that he would assume that was you and I that had taken the room. Your theory sounds plausible but do you think that that Andy, whatever his name was, would take the risk of waiting to see what we would do? What if we hadn't taken them to the jeweller? What makes you think that we knew where to take them? And come to think of it, how did Joe's body come to be in the Clyde near Glasgow?"
"You're right, clever girl. As a detective I make a good mechanic. However, I'm still a little worried about that diamond I sold."
"Well we've finished our lunch and I think that we can worry about those things later", Liz said. "Meanwhile let's go and look at our room." Howard did not miss the wink she gave him.

CHAPTER TWENTY-FOUR

Detective Inspector Alistair McIntosh felt annoyed that what he had thought was going to be an army problem was now beginning to look like being a long-drawn-out murder case for him to solve. He was convinced that it would certainly delay his retirement.
After the girl's boy friend at the Naval Air Station had been interviewed he had also dismissed the possibility that the murdered American soldier had had anything to do with the one who had been arrested at Carlisle. However, he now knew that the girl had known more about this G.I. than she had told the Carlisle police at the time and that probably went for the sailor as well. But why had the murdered victim got off the train at Carlisle when he had told them that he was going to Glasgow? What had happened to him after that? Did he ever get to Glasgow before he was murdered? Why should anyone strangle him and put his body into the Clyde? Perhaps all this would become clear when he was able to question that girl and her sailor boy friend together.
The inspector called his sergeant into his office. "Have you made all those enquiries I asked you to do, Baillie?"
"I have sir - just finished them. I did the last phone call about two minutes ago."
"Well, don't mess about man. What have you found out?"
"I've discovered that the girl stayed at the Renfield Hotel in St. Enoch's Square for four nights was not joined by this sailor chap Hartwell until Tuesday evening. The hotel understood that they were married."
"Hmm! Now we know that's not true."
"The clerk told me that the lady had said that the room had been booked wrongly in her maiden name of Harrison but was now married and changed it to Hartwell."
"Who'd booked the room?"
"It had been booked in advance of their arrival by a Scottish soldier named..." the sergeant opened his notebook and flipped over a couple of pages, "McKern who had his arm in a sling. He booked the room in the name of Mr and Mrs Harrison.

Alistair leant back in his chair and folded his arms. "I don't think I need three guesses who they were. I think she travelled from London with this American Joe Peabody and the room was booked in her name to disguise who the American was.
"Now I wonder why that was done, Baillie? And who is this man McKern?" Then, when she thought she'd seen him arrested on Carlisle Station she paired up with the sailor to take his place."
"But they only had one night together." Sergeant Baillie observed.
"Probably it was the only night he could get a pass out. Had you thought of that? Did you also check whether that Joe Peabody stayed at the hotel as the same time of Hartwell and the girl? If not he must have gone somewhere else or perhaps he never left Carlisle"
"I did check that too sir. The only G.I. that was there about the same time was a fella called Mitchell He also left on Wednesday without paying his bill but they thought that he might be coming back as he'd left some personal things in his room, but he didn't.
"Didn't what?"
"Didn't come back sir. The clerk told me that when he arrived on Saturday he asked to see the register and commented on the fact that the name of Harrison had been deleted. I believe Mitchell could have been this Mr Harrison who was really someone else. He enquired about the Hartwells who had booked the room and apparently waited until he saw, who the clerk described as Elizabeth Hartwell, come in but never approached her. He also said that he never ever saw them together the whole time they were both in the hotel. If fact it appeared, according to the clerk, that he tried to avoid her altogether."
"So you think that this Mr Harrison was really Joe Peabody?" asked the Inspector. "Why would he change his name to Mitchell d'ya think? and then not want to see her? But go on Baillie, what about the girl?"
"Well, she left suddenly on Wednesday evening, probably after an argument, leaving the sailor with a huge amount of money owing to the hotel. Hartwell actually stayed on for another night. What is mysterious sir, is that first he sold a diamond to a dealer he met in

the hotel to pay the bill."
"Did you say a diamond, Sergeant? What sort of a diamond? Do you mean a diamond ring?"
"The manager said it was just a diamond. He didn't mention a ring."
"People don't just carry diamonds around with them Sergeant, least of all Fleet Air Arm Mechanics! You'd better check on that. What else?"
"Well, what I don't understand is that if Mitchell was Joe Peabody then why didn't he make himself known to the girl and what reason could he have for not doing so?"
"Perhaps the secret lies with this soldier, what's his name...?"
"McKern, sir, Andy McKern. I believe."
"Yes, McKern, Sergeant. But I would like you to find out why the room was booked in the name of Harrison, the girl's maiden name. The key to this could be why this American Joe Peabody didn't want anyone to know he was going to be there. It might have been that he was in fear of something happening to him."
"Which it did!" the sergeant interjected and then added, "I expect that the girl will be able to tell us that when we question her."
"Where is this soldier who booked the room I wonder? Could he be somewhere locally or perhaps just on leave? The hotel clerk did say that he had his arm in a sling. And where did Hartwell get that diamond? Two questions, and maybe more, need answering Baillie, or are we on some wild goose chase? Perhaps none of them had anything to do with this murdered American? We know from the landlord at the pub where she worked that the girl, Elizabeth Harrison, is single and she told him that she was going to Glasgow to see her sick aunt - that is if one exists," the inspector said as an afterthought. "Has anyone found the girl yet?"
"Well yes I think so."
"What do you mean, 'you think so'? Have you or haven't you?"

"She's been seen by the Duty Guard at the camp, who saw her meet our sailor friend..."
Inspector Alistair McIntosh interrupted his sergeant, "Don't call

him our friend, Baillie, he could be our murderer, but go on."
"Well, nothing else really. She met him and they had a long talk at the camp entrance and then she went off."
"Do you mean you've lost her Baillie?"
"I'm afraid we have sir, but the guard heard them say that they arranged to meet but he missed where and Hartwell left the camp soon afterwards on a 48 hour pass out. I could go back and question him again sir, when he goes back on board."
Inspector McIntosh looked at his sergeant in disbelief. "On board Baillie? It's not a ship!" Since when have you been using nautical terms? It's an airfield!"
"I think in the Fleet Air Arm they call it a concrete aircraft-carrier sir. 'Back on board' is a phrase they use when..."
Alistair again interrupted him. "I know all that sergeant, for goodness sake get on with it."
"There's nothing left to tell sir. We'll have to wait until he goes back and hopefully she will turn up as well."
The inspector held his head in despair. "What a way to run an enquiry!" and then added sarcastically, "I suppose you're waiting for that mysterious Scotsman who booked them into the hotel to also just turn up are you, sergeant? What's his name? McKern isn't it? Have you tried the War Office, Baillie?"
"There must be hundreds of McKerns, sir."
"Well you've got to start somewhere. It's no good sitting around here for forty-eight hours..." Alistair stopped what he was going to say as he suddenly thought of an idea. "Tell you what, sergeant, while you're waiting, go out and make inquiries at all the jewellers' shops in Glasgow. If diamonds are part of this jigsaw, then a local jeweller may know something. Try the back street ones first."
Alistair considered that he was not making much progress but perhaps his sergeant would discover some clues in the enquiries he was to make among the jewellers. He still believed that the most important key to this murder could be that the girl. She not only travelled with this Joe Peabody but knew him well, which is not what she told the police at Carlisle. According to the landlord

of the pub where she worked, he heard his barmaid mentioning a soldier with that name and suspected that she had met Joe in London and they had travelled together to Glasgow.
He believed that his sergeant had been right when he concluded that it seemed they had intended to have a few days together at the Renfield hotel and the sailor had grabbed the opportunity to take his place after they thought that they had seen him arrested. It seemed to him to be obvious that either she had suggested it or she would not have needed much persuasion.
Perhaps Howard Hartwell's diamond was nothing to do with the murder but he had to follow up every possibility. He swore quietly at his sergeant's incompetence of not organising a twenty-four hour watch on the Naval Station, which had allowed the girl to slip through their fingers and subsequently further delay the investigation. His retirement now seemed much further away than it did a week ago.

CHAPTER TWENTY-FIVE

Late the next morning Sergeant Baillie entered the jeweller's owned by Charlie MacKenzie. He had already visited about half the shops on his list and had the rest to do in the afternoon. He introduced himself and took out Joe's photograph that the police had been given.
"You've no doubt seen the report in all the papers of a murdered American soldier..."
Charlie shook his head. He said that he never bought newspapers. He considered them a waste of money when the wireless could give him all the news that he wanted to know. The sergeant noticed the jeweller's negative response but carried on to ask the question that he had put to all the others as he showed him the photograph.
"Have you seen this American soldier before and has he ever visited your shop?"
Charlie went pale as he looked at the photograph. In a moment, he relived the events of a fortnight or so earlier. Charlie shook his head again, "No, no, I've never seen him before," he lied, not very convincingly he thought. Charlie wasn't very good at lying and Sergeant Baillie looked as if he didn't believe him. He could see the drops of perspiration on the shopkeeper's forehead and upper lip.
"This man's body was found in the Clyde near Bothwell. He'd been in the water some time Mr MacKenzie. We want to find out who killed him." He looked closely at the slightly bent, white-haired man. "It would help if you could remember if he came into your shop to buy or sell you something. Can you recall when he came here?"
Sergeant Baillie was an experienced policeman. He knew his job and he knew that this was the time to keep quiet. He had asked an important question and waited for an answer.
At first, Charlie thought that the policeman had known that Joe had been there but as he had not told him how the American had died, he had to be careful that he didn't let on what he knew about

his death. Perhaps they thought that he had just drowned. The only problem was that he had to tell another lie.
"Let me have another look at that photograph." Charlie held out his hand to take the photograph off the sergeant. He felt calmer now. "No, I don't remember him. Why? What's he done to get murdered?"
"That's what we're trying to find out. Are you absolutely sure that you do not recognise this man and that he has never been here try to sell you a diamond or two?"
The word 'diamonds' took Charlie by surprise. His hand began to shake a little which he steadied by placing it on the counter. "I'm absolutely sure officer. Were they stolen? I never handle stolen goods."
"I'll ask the questions if you don't mind, sir." Sergeant Baillie considered leaving at that point and bringing in the inspector, but then re-considered the situation, feeling capable enough of handling it himself. "Why did you ask if they were stolen?"
"I supposed that's why you asked me that question officer. After all you wouldn't be here unless you knew that someone was trying to sell them when they weren't his to sell." Suddenly Charlie felt a little calmer but wondered whether the sergeant knew more than he was prepared to tell him. "I just thought that's why he'd been murdered." Using the word 'murdered' caused his voice to shake a little. Thankfully the sergeant did not appear to notice and dismissed Charlie's comments putting his nervousness down to his age.
The sergeant began to think that perhaps no jeweller in the City had been involved and that his Inspector was wrong in thinking that. "One final question sir. Do you know anyone by the name of McKern, a soldier?"
Charlie felt his mouth go dry. Should he lie yet again. He wasn't going to admit that he had known Andy for as many years as he cared to remember but wondered if the police might find out that he used to be friendly with him before he went into the army.
"I did know a chap with that name who used to work in Glasgow before the war, but he went into the army and I haven't seen him

since." Charlie was surprised how convincing his own voice had sounded and how calmly he had answered the sergeant's question.
Sergeant Baillie closed his notebook and put away the photograph. "If we need to ask you any more questions we'll be back."
When the policeman had gone Charlie went to the back of the shop and poured himself a generous tot of Johnny Walker's Black label whisky which he kept all through the war for special occasions and he considered that this had been one of them. They obviously wanted to find Andy McKern and he feared that if they found out that Andy was implicated in Joe's murder he would also be in trouble. He would have liked to have told the policeman all he knew but didn't know how to do it without involving himself. He drank his whisky quickly and poured himself another double.

Later that afternoon Liz and Howard waited until the shop was empty before entering. Charlie looked up and the blood drained from his face. It was the second shock that he had that day. He could tell by the expression on their faces that they had not come to congratulate him or renew acquaintances. Howard pulled down the blind on the door and suggested that Charlie should lock it. Charlie made no objection but collected his keys from the back of the shop and did as he was told. He knew that he would be forced to tell what had taken place after he had told his visitors that the diamonds were worthless.
"Now, Charlie, we want to know the truth. As you probably know Joe's been found dead." Charlie nodded his head and Howard continued without pausing, "and we believe that you know what happened. We reckon that we brought you real diamonds and you lied to us that they were paste doing us out a lot of money. We want to know why and what you hoped to gain and, for that matter, what you know about Joe's death."
Charlie put up both his hands to stop him. "I've already had the police here this morning and told them nothing but I have to tell someone what I know otherwise I'll go mad." He still felt a little light-headed after drinking the whisky and also that he could not

lie anymore. "If I tell you, it'll perhaps ensure that I'll have a good night's rest for the first time since it happened. You'd better come to the back of the shop and sit down. It's a long story."

CHAPTER TWENTY-SIX

A few days ago Detective Chief Inspector Alistair McIntosh had been looking forward to his retirement but now his old ulcer was beginning to play him up. He stirred a spoonful of bicarbonate of soda into some milk, which he drank before addressing his sergeant.

"OK, Baillie, let's sort this out. What do have so far? We have a bloke called Joe Peabody, an American Army soldier, who was travelling with his girl Elizabeth Harrison, on his way to Glasgow for a dirty weekend. We know that a chap called Andy McKern had already booked a room for them at the Renfield Hotel, but we don't know who he is or what his connections are with the American. This girl sees the American arrested as a deserter when he gets off the train at Carlisle and assumes that she won't see him ever again. Disappointed, she puts on her charms to a sailor who is travelling in the same compartment. He naturally can't resist the advances of a pretty girl and they take up the room at the hotel that Joe would have had. He must have thought that he was on a good thing and that all his Christmases had come at once. A beautiful girl and the chance to spend a few days in a hotel with her would be too good to refuse.

Unfortunately it appears that he could only get one night's leave, which apparently didn't work out very well. But when she told the police at Carlisle that she was travelling with her sailor boyfriend and that she didn't know who Joe was, we now know she was lying, but as she had a reason to do so we'll give her the benefit of the doubt. I'll be kind to her and say that she was bending the truth."

Sergeant Baillie looked please about that bit of generosity by his superior.

"But the mystery still is that this Joe Peabody..." the inspector shook his head, " Peabody! What a name for anyone to carry around...must have seen them but didn't make himself known!"

"He could have had a good reason for doing so sir but one that we

don't know about yet."
"Did you say that the porter told you that an American left the hotel on Wednesday evening and never came back?"
"I think so sir."
"But isn't that the same time when the girl left the hotel sergeant?"
"Yes it is. But surely you're not suggesting that Elizabeth Harrison strangled Joe then took him to Bothwell and put him in the Clyde before catching the train back to London!"
"Do I look that stupid sergeant? I was wondering that if Joe came to Glasgow for another reason and had arranged to meet the soldier McKern, he might then wish to keep a low profile. I think that we need to question that soldier McKern urgently."
"Perhaps his original intention of bringing the girl with him was a blind to cover what he and McKern had planned to do, so when he discovered that she was shacking up with Hartwell he didn't mind too much as she was now off his hands."
"Probably so sergeant, but may I remind you that you still haven't found Elizabeth Harrison yet. We need some answers from her as well, including why she left so abruptly leaving Hartwell to pay the hotel bill with that mystery diamond."
Baillie looked puzzled. "I wonder why he did that sir. Shouldn't we find out how he came to have a diamond in his pocket? I can't question him at the moment. I'll do so when I go to the aircraft ca..." the sergeant nearly added the word 'carrier', but remembered how his inspector had reacted last time he used the Fleet Air Arm name for the Naval Air Station and quickly changed it to..."the airfield."
Alistair looked at his sergeant in disbelief." Why can't you question him? Where is he? You haven't lost HIM now?"
"I understand that he's taken a few days leave and no one knows where he's gone, except that I think he's gone off with that girl Elizabeth Harrison."
"I don't believe it!" The inspector put his head in his hands. "What about the jewellers then Baillie? Any success there?"
"No sir. No one saw or knew either the American or McKern or had dealt with diamonds recently. There was one old man who I

thought knew more than he told me at first but he is not the sort of person to murder anybody. He was a nice old boy really, but I think that I frightened him."
"You're not supposed to think sergeant you're supposed to act and your next move is to find that soldier McKern."

After Charlie MacKenzie had explained to Elizabeth and Howard what took place that night when they had left the shop, they wondered how this quiet little man could have been party to everything that had happened. Firstly, the deceit he had perpetrated on behalf of those criminals and, secondly, the way that he had been able to convince them that the real diamonds were fakes and worthless. However, Liz suddenly began to feel sorry for this pathetic old man. Joe's brutal murder had placed him in an unenviable position. He would not be able to tell the police about how Joe had been murdered for fear of what might happen to him if he did, especially after keeping quiet about it all this time.
"But you haven't done badly out if it," Howard said. "I suppose that you still have the diamonds or have benefited from their value by selling them."
Charlie shook his head. "I've never made any money from the diamonds. They are all in a safe deposit box in my bank and the money I paid out has left me with a huge overdraft. I can't even bear to look at the stones let alone sell them to the trade. So what good has it done me? I see Joe's murder in my dreams every night since - that is when I'm able to get any sleep at all."
Liz and Howard had gone to the shop feeling sorry for themselves at being swindled out of a fortune but they didn't envy the old man's plight. Indeed, Howard began to wonder how they could help him.
"Where are these two fellows, McKern and his mate?" Howard asked. "Do you know?"
"I expect they could be traced quite easily if they haven't left the army or deserted. Andy told me that he was going to have some hospital treatment for his arm. I believe the surgeons were going

to try and repair it for him."
"What was wrong with his arm?" Liz asked.
"He'd been shot in the shoulder and his nerves were damaged. It could be that he's had his operation last week."
Liz looked at Howard, "If it was that bad he might have needed a few operations. We could go round to the hospitals and make enquiries."
Charlie looked worried. "Now, hold on a minute you two. If the police find him he's bound to try and save his own skin by telling them that his mate killed Joe. Then the police will find out about the diamonds and I'll be in serious trouble. I can't risk it. Leave it alone and go back home. I'll give you five hundred pounds each if you forget it. It will help to compensate you both for what you've lost or what I did you out of. Tell the police nothing. Don't worry about me. I feel better already now that I've told somebody."
"We'll think about it and come and see you again before we go."
Liz clung on to Howard's arm as they left the shop. "What are we going to do Howard? We can't leave it like this, but I'm thrilled about the money he's promised us to keep quiet."

The next day Howard was due back at the Naval Station and Liz walked with him down the narrow road alongside the river Cart in the early morning sunshine. What they did not expect to see was a uniformed policeman coming out of the guardroom as they approached the gates.
"Air Mechanic Hartwell?" the policeman looked very serious. "There are some questions we'd like to ask you.
He turned to look at Elizabeth. "And you'll be Miss Harrison. Am I right, miss?"
"You're quite right officer. I suppose you want to talk to me as well."
"Not me, miss. I've already been in touch with the CID in Glasgow when I saw the two of you coming down the road and they're sending a car. Perhaps you'll be good enough to wait here until they arrive."
"Have we any choice?" Howard remarked grinning at Liz.

When the car eventually arrived Sergeant Baillie was in the front seat. He got out and approached the couple.
"I would like you both to come with me to the police station, if you would please. Detective Inspector McIntosh wants to ask you some questions about that American G.I. who was found dead."
Howard grinned again at Liz. "Everyone's being very polite about it," he said to her, and then, turning to the sergeant, he teased, "What if we refused?"
"Ah, then I would have to arrest you on suspicion of being involved in the murder of Private Joseph Peabody, sir and you wouldn't want that would you sir, especially not the young lady?" The sergeant looked at Liz and gave her a kindly smile.
"You must be joking," Howard said in a voice that sounded as though he was dismissing the suggestion.
"It would be best if you save what you have to say until we get to the station I think sir."
Howard shrugged his shoulders, resigning himself to the inevitable as they both got into the back seat of the car

CHAPTER TWENTY-SEVEN

Andy McKern was in the Glasgow Royal Infirmary recovering from the operation on his shoulder to try and repair the damage that had been done by that German sniper's bullet. He thought that at first he would probably have to lose his arm but the doctors had told him that there was a good chance that they might be able to save it.

He opened his locker and took out an old "Daily Mirror" which had been in there for some time. He had not felt like reading it before because of the pain he was suffering, but he was now feeling much better. After glancing at the headlines, he turned to the centre pages. Joe's face stared at him just below the story of how the body had been discovered in the Clyde. His heart missed a beat and then, as he read that the police were appealing for witnesses, he relaxed a little when he realised that the only two were his friend Sid, who had helped him dispose of the body after killing him and Charlie MacKenzie the jeweller who had seen the murder take place.

The story in the paper told how Joe had been identified from his tag, which was still round his neck when the police found him. He could not understand how both he and Sid had forgotten to remove it but could not even remember thinking about it at the time. It could only have been that they had been so anxious to dispose of the body as soon as they had the opportunity to do so. That chance had presented itself unexpectedly when they crossed the bridge at Bothwell on their way back to Carlisle.

He remembered how they had first quickly tied the body but obviously not very securely, to a lump of concrete that they had found in a bombed building nearby, then dropped the corpse into the river from the bridge. There had been no traffic to speak of on the road at that late hour and fortunately it had been a very dark night. They had parked their vehicle close to the bridge, knowing that it would not have been given a second glance by anyone passing by, because people had been so used to seeing army transport on the road late at night and, in any case, very few

people had a car. Even if any other vehicle had passed by at the time it would have been almost impossible to have connected their vehicle with the murder The police had also stated in the newspaper that they did not know exactly when the body was dumped. Andy felt sure that because of these reasons he would not be able to be traced.
Later that afternoon he had an unexpected visitor.
Corporal Sidney Cope stood at the bottom of Andy's bed looking very serious.
"What the hell are you doing here Sid? I thought we'd agreed nae to be seen together."
"I found out where you were from your neighbour in the tenement block. She told me that you were in hospital but I've had a long job finding out which bloody hospital!"
"You hinna been roon' to my flat, you silly sod! We're nae supposed to ken one another!"
Sidney dismissed Andy's rebuke. "Have you seen the papers? They've found that bloody American."
Andy looked round to see if anyone had heard him. "Why don't you keep your damn voice doon? Do you want the whole ward to hear yer? I've seen the story and I dinna ken what you're worried aboot. Anyway, who's going to tell the polis' aboot anything? Charlie won't split. He'll lose his fuckin' diamonds if he did and I'm jist waiting to spend that money which I hinna even touched yet."
"Don't be stupid," Sid remarked. "Have you forgotten about that girl of Joe's that you twisted out of her fortune? What's she got to lose if she tells the police about what Joe was carrying? If she's got any brains she'll put two and two together and realise that you've pinched the money and now that Joe's body's been found, presume that you bloody well killed him."
Andy jumped in quickly before Sid could say any more. "If she finds out what happened at Charlie's place, the polis' will question Charlie 'til they get the truth and then you'll be in fuckin' trouble."
"The best thing you can do is to get out of here as soon as you can and disappear," Sid said.

"Why should I dae that? I fuckin' well dinna kill Joe, you fuckin' did!"
It was now Sid's turn to look around in case anyone else was listening. "And you're an accomplice and don't you forget it chum. When are you likely to get out of this bloody hole?"
"When they tell me. The doctor's coming today to tell me what's happening. I'm beginning to get some feeling in me fingers again."
"You'll get some feeling in your bloody neck when the rope is round it if we're not careful. I think we'd better lie low until this thing blows over. Tell that quack of yours that you want to go home and then we'll get together and sort this thing out."
After his unwelcome visitor had left Andy worried about his half of the money that he had hidden in his flat together with his own £4000. He knew Sid too well to be able to trust him. He had to get out of the hospital as quickly as possible.

CHAPTER TWENTY-EIGHT

Chief Inspector Alistair McIntosh went over the papers in the case of Joe Peabody's murder yet again and still not sure whether he had all the information he wanted. He waited patiently for his sergeant to arrive with Howard Hartwell and Elizabeth Harrison. The war department had sent the inspector the information he had requested about Andy McKern, together with details about the wound to his arm and the instructions he had been given to attend the Royal Infirmary in Glasgow for treatment.
However, when enquiries had been made at the hospital the previous evening, it was found that he had discharged himself the day before and he was not at the Glasgow address they had been given by the hospital which was obviously false.
When asked whether McKern had had any visitors the hospital confirmed that there had been one the day before McKern discharged himself in the same type of uniform as their patient.
The police had been supplied with the name of this other soldier who apparently was stationed at the same Barracks as McKern in Carlisle. The inspector looked again at the papers and read the name Corporal Sidney Cope. Following the police request for information as to the movements of these men, he discovered that this other soldier had used an army vehicle to take some things to a depot in Glasgow two or three weeks ago, returning the following day. He didn't think he needed to pursue this, as he considered that this other soldier would be nothing to do with his inquiry.

However, Chief Inspector Alistair McIntosh's mind was on the two people his sergeant was bringing in.
Howard and Liz came into his room followed by Sergeant Baillie. The inspector was taken aback when he saw how good-looking she was. He smiled and, unusually for him, was lost for words for a minute or two. Finally he found his voice. "So we meet at last, Miss Harrison."
"I didn't think I was so important that you needed to seek me out."

"Well, there are some questions I want to ask you with regard to this inquiry and into the circumstances of this American soldier's death. Apart from just being a fellow traveller on the train, you knew this Joe Peabody didn't you?"
Elizabeth hesitated for a second before answering, "Yes, I did."
The inspector was silent for a moment. He had expected her to deny it. He shuffled through the papers on his desk and selected a document, which he waved at her. "But you told the Carlisle police when you made enquiries about an American soldier that he was just someone who you'd met on the train and that your boyfriend was this man," he pointed to Howard.
"Well, that wasn't quite right. I had known Joe for some months and when he came back from Europe he told me that he had to see someone in Scotland. He had apparently arranged for a soldier he'd met on the boat coming over, to book a room in a hotel in Glasgow and we'd have a few nights together. I didn't love Joe but he always excited me."
The sergeant was smiling at her all this time. He was thinking that he wouldn't have minded a bit of excitement with her himself. He heard the inspector's voice booming at him.
"Sergeant, are you writing all this down?" Then, turning back to the girl, he said with a sarcastic tone in his voice, "Go on, your story is fascinating."
Sergeant Baillie glared at his inspector and thought how unkindly he had spoken to her. Liz was glad of the break. Although she had rehearsed this story with Howard, it gave her time to think what she was saying and to get the rest of the story right. Most of it was true anyway.
"I suspected that he'd come over without permission, or whatever it's called and when Howard and I saw Joe being arrested - or rather who we thought was Joe - the last thing I wanted to do was to get involved. After talking it over with Howard," she turned towards him and squeezed his hand - "he has been marvellous, by the way, though all this - I decided to change the name in the register to Howard's name and pretend that he was my husband.
"After a few days I was lonely, so I went to the camp and

arranged to meet him, and you probably know the rest."
The inspector was listening very carefully to everything she had to say. "Go on," he said. He was half beginning to believe her story and wanted to see if it tallied with what they had already found out.
"Well, we spent Tuesday night together and arranged to have another night but we had a disagreement..." Sergeant Baillie thought that he saw her bottom lip tremble a little, "and I...." Liz tried to continue and managed to find a tear and let it run down her cheek. "I'm sorry Inspector, but now that we've found each other again, we've fallen in love, and I really don't want to talk about the time when I left him in the lurch. I thought he would hate me for it at the time, but he's forgiven me now." She wiped the tear from her cheek with her finger.
The sergeant was already close by her side and handed her his handkerchief to dry her eyes.
The inspector became a little agitated. None of this was leading him any nearer to solving the murder. He was not fully convinced that the girl was telling him the truth, but now he was intrigued to discover why Howard had a diamond in his pocket..
"Mr Hartwell, we've since discovered that you paid the Bill at the hotel with a diamond. Perhaps you will tell me...."
The door to his office opened abruptly and a young constable stood there, "Sorry to interrupt you sir but some very important information has just been 'phoned through with regard to this case you are investigating. I thought that you should know."
The inspector looked towards the two he had been questioning as he prepared to leave the room. "You will excuse me. I'll be back in a minute."
"Now what is it constable? What's so important? I'm in the middle of a murder enquiry."
"I'm aware of that sir, but the body of that soldier you wanted to interview has been found inside a flat in a tenement building in a back street in the Gorbals district."
Chief Inspector McIntosh went back into the room and turned to Liz and Howard. "You can go for the present but I'll want to talk

to you both again," then, walking briskly to the door, he grabbed his sergeant's arm. "Right Baillie, we're going visiting."

When they were in the car, Alistair explained to his sergeant where they were going. "I think I now know who, but I'm damned if I know why!" he added.
When they arrived at the building a sole policeman stood at the open door of the flat. McKern was face down on the floor in a crumpled heap. The room was in state of untidiness. Drawers were open and the contents strewn about all over the place.
"Looks as if he's been robbed," Sergeant Baillie observed. "Unless the murderer was looking for something in particular. What do you think sir?"
Alistair ignored the question but turned to the constable on duty, "Who found the body?"
"It was the lady next door sir. She saw the door open when she came to go out shopping. She doesn't remember hearing anything but said that she probably wouldn't because she is a little deaf. There's no blood, sir, so I think he must have been struck down..."
Alistair interrupted him, "Thank you constable, we'll leave the analysis to the experts if you don't mind."
More police arrived and then the pathologist. Turning to his sergeant he added, "Nothing else we can do here Baillie, we'll leave so that they can get on with doing whatever they have to do. Meanwhile, let's get back to the station. I want you to make a couple of telephone calls."
He looked towards the pathologist. "I expect you won't be long here. After you've got this laddie back to the mortuary, I'll meet you there in about an hour or so. Is that enough time for you?"
"Yes I think so. Looks pretty straightforward to me. He bent down to examine the body. "Reckon he died about midnight."

An hour-and-a-half later the Chief Inspector was at the hospital mortuary talking to the pathologist.
"You're making a habit of these kind of corpses, Alistair This is the second one you've given me inside a fortnight with the same

cause of death."
"Strangled?" Alistair asked.
"Well, sort of. I believe that the cause of death was roughly the same as the last one, but this one's easier to detect as he's only been dead since about midnight, as I told you at the flat and not as bad a state as the last one was in. This one died as a result of cardiac shock from compression of the neck ganglia."
"You mean strangled," repeated the inspector.
"Well that's the simplest way to describe it. The important thing is that someone would have to know exactly what to do to kill this laddie quickly."
"Bit like last time then. Do you think the same person did both murders?"
"Could be. It's most unusual to find two people murdered in the same way close to each other. It's just a question of making sure the killer got the right place on the neck to exert the pressure. If I had to guess I would say he's probably a soldier who's been trained to kill."
"Well you can leave the guessing to me but I thought it might be the same one."
"By the way, Alistair, did you know that we found a one-hundred pound note under the body?"

CHAPTER TWENTY-NINE

As the inspector made his way back to the station, he knew now that it had been a case of robbery, but a one-hundred pound note was an awful lot of money and there must have been more in the flat. He wondered what his sergeant would have to tell him from the telephone calls he had asked him to make.
When he arrived at the station Sergeant Baillie followed him into his room. "You were quite right, sir. That friend of the deceased, Corporal Cope, is on a three days' leave. He's due back later today.
"Did you tell them to detain him when he gets back and that we want to question him?"
Baillie nodded. "If he did both the murders then what was his motive?"
"Robbery I think, but we'll have to wait to find out when we arrest him."
"Arrest him? Does that mean we'll be going all the way to Carlisle, sir?"
"That's why I asked you to make that third telephone call sergeant. What did you find out?"
"There is a slow train at five o'clock, or there's the overnight express to London which stops at Carlisle and leaves at nine, otherwise we'll have to wait until tomorrow morning."
"Well done Baillie. It all depends on what we hear from the Commanding Officer at the Barracks."

Later that afternoon, the inspector received a telephone call from the Camp Commandant of the Army Camp at Carlisle.
"Major Corkingdale here, Inspector. I'm afraid I have some bad news for you. That Corporal Cope you wanted to question. Dead, I'm afraid. Silly ass went berserk when we told him that you wanted to question him about a murder. Snatched a loaded gun from one of the M.Ps and tried to commandeer an army staff car. One of the MPs shot at him to wound him and to try and prevent him from getting away. Missed his aim I'm afraid and shot him

straight through the heart. Quite accidental of course. There'll be a stink about it. Shouldn't have done it, naturally, but he reacted quickly when he saw the gun pointing at him. Very sorry Inspector but I do have some good news for you."
Chief Inspector Alistair McIntosh could not believe his ears. His only suspect dead! What news could there be that was good? "What's the good news?" he asked, feeling completely dejected.
"Found almost £19,000 in old notes in a bag he was carrying. All large notes. An absolute fortune! No doubt that's why he didn't want to be arrested and tried to get away. Is that what you wanted him for Inspector? Did he rob a bank or something and kill someone in the process? He was trained for it. One of our best men at one time, mark you. Such a lot of money. What do you want me to do with it? God! What a mess!"
Alistair was lost for words. £19,000! He had to think. "Can I call you back Major? I'll try and tell you what's to be done as soon as I've consulted my Chief."
Alistair knew that his Chief Superintendent would have to be told all about this, but first, he thought that he had better try and sort it out. There was now no point in dashing off to Carlisle and Cope had confirmed his suspicions that he had murdered his friend McKern by trying to run away when he was told why he was wanted for questioning. The money he had in his possession, which he had no doubt stolen from McKern after he had killed him, was yet another reason for running away and it solved his problem about motive - but who gave Andy McKern all that money? £19,000 was, after all, an awful lot! If Cope had also killed the American before dumping him into the Clyde it was probably because Joe Peabody had the money in the first place at that had been the reason for him coming to Glasgow.
"Well Baillie, what do you think?" Alistair looked closely at his sergeant after telling him all that the Major had told him.
Sergeant Baillie was an uncomplicated man and invariably looked for a simple solution to everything. However he could not imagine what £19,000 looked like but wondered where on earth all that amount of money could have come from, or why it had been in

that soldier's possession.
"Do you think he might have been holding it for somebody sir? If he had intended to keep it for himself he must have left the hospital with the intention of clearing off with it, then that chap Cope must have known about it and killed him for it. Do you think that's what happened, sir"
"It certainly seems something like that, but you have made an important observation sergeant. Perhaps he was waiting to see if the operations on his arm were successful before disappearing but go on, think, man."
"The girl might know more than she has told us already, sir? If she knew that the American was carrying money for McKern then she wouldn't have admitted it for fear of incriminating herself."
"Now you're getting warm sergeant. Remember the American, Joseph Peabody, was killed in the same way as Andy McKern."
"Of course sir. Perhaps McKern knew that the American had the money and told his pal Cope, who killed him. McKern kept the money safe until he came out of hospital, but Cope murdered him for it...no sir, that can't be right. Why was there any need to kill anybody? And if the American was carrying all that money where was he taking it to? Perhaps he picked it up in Carlisle, sir"
The Chief Inspector looked thoughtful. "We will never know what really happened as there is no one to question. The three men who seem to have been involved are all dead. But you've confirmed my theory, Baillie. I think we've got the story about right, but not the details and there are still a few questions left unanswered. Let's have that girl in again with Hartwell. Mind you I don't think the Navy fellow had anything to do with it. I think that she picked him up on the train as she said she did after she thought that her American boyfriend had been arrested."

When Liz and Howard returned to the police station they were both very nervous and apprehensive as to what questions they were going to be asked. Howard had thought up what he considered to be an answer to the inspector's inevitable question of where he had obtained that diamond which he had sold at the

hotel. However, the inspector began by asking Liz a different question. He thrust a one hundred pound note across the table towards her. "What do you know about this?"
Liz immediately guessed that it was from the money that had been paid in exchange for the diamonds. "Nothing. I've never seen a one hundred pound note before. Where did you get it?" she asked, trying to sound innocent of any knowledge about the money.
"That Scottish soldier friend of your American has also been found strangled here in Glasgow. The note was found in his flat where he had been murdered."
"Surely you don't think that we..."
The inspector interrupted her. "No Miss Harrison. We know that neither of you are anything to do with Joe's murder. However, we're pretty certain that we know who the murderer was and now he's dead. There has been a lot of money involved and we're trying to find but where it all came from. Do you think that your late friend, G.I. Joe Peabody, might have been carrying some money when you were travelling with him on the train?"
The inspector's question had told her that the police knew nothing about the diamonds thank goodness and although she had gasped at the news that both soldiers were dead, she was not too upset. Their deaths would mean that there was now nobody left alive who knew about the diamonds apart from themselves and the jeweller Charlie MacKenzie,
"Now you've mentioned it, Inspector, he did tell me something about arranging a money transaction when he got to Glasgow, but as far as I remember he took nothing with him when he got off the train at Carlisle. We didn't find anything that he'd left in the compartment, did we, Howard?"
Howard shook his head in confirmation. "But I'd never really thought about that until you just reminded me of it," she added.
Howard was confused as he listened to Liz lying to the police officers, but found himself nodding in agreement at her answer to the Inspector’s question. She must know what she is doing, he thought, and her story sounded so believable. The inspector leaned across the table, picked up the note and waved in front of her face.

"And who did he say he was he taking it to? Was it that soldier?"
"I've just told you that I don't know anything about him having any money with him. If he had told me what he was going to do when he arrived in Glasgow I would have remembered about the money before now. So - I'm afraid - the answer is... I don't know." And then she added, to try to stop him questioning her further, "I was just looking forward to an exciting few days. I really know nothing about any money."
The inspector sat very still, staring at her, trying to read into her eyes whether or not she was telling the truth. After what seemed to Liz to be an eternity he leaned back in his chair smiling to himself. He suspected that she was lying about something but he was convinced that they had nothing to do with the murders. "Right, you can both go now. I doubt if I'll need to see you again."
Howard grabbed Liz firmly by the arm as he hurried her out of the building.
"What's the rush, Howard? Where are you taking me?"
"It was that one-hundred pound note which reminded me," Howard said excitedly. "Have you forgotten that MacKenzie offered us five-hundred pounds each if we told the police nothing - and we haven't, so let's go and pick up that money before it's too late."

CHAPTER THIRTY

Chief Inspector McIntosh could not wait to call his sergeant back into his office. "I think I've got it," he announced. "Listen to me sergeant and tell me if I've got it wrong."
"Before you start, sir, I took another call from that Major at the camp. He said that they've searched Corporal Cope's things and found another huge sum of money. Another £15,000!"
The inspector raised both of his hands and looked relieved. "Good man, Baillie. You've just supplied the missing link. There's no doubt in my mind that Cope did both murders. The motive was the old one - greed. Now how about this?"
Sergeant Baillie wondered what he was about to say.
"I believe that the American was going to Glasgow to pick up the money on the following Wednesday and used his girl friend to cover-up the real reason for his journey. The meeting at Carlisle had been arranged previously without telling Miss Harrison why he needed to see that Andy McKern. He obviously intended to re-board the train and carry on to Glasgow with his girl friend. For some reason he didn't do it. It may have been the incident that happened on the platform when that other U.S. soldier was arrested, or McKern had been late turning up, or for some other reason."
Sergeant Baillie looked a little puzzled. "But if the American didn't need his girl friend, why did he stay at the same hotel and keep a watch on her and the sailor and, according to the desk clerk, also sound annoyed when he found out they were pretending to be a honeymoon couple."
"For the sole reason to have some fun and then embarrass her when he collected the money before revealing himself and, also have the satisfaction of kicking the sailor to kingdom come. Then he would probably give her some of the money as he had planned to do all along before taking her back to Dorset."
He waited for some reaction from his sergeant. "If that was so why didn't he promise her some of it beforehand?"
"We will never know what his intentions were. But to return to

my theory. I don't understand the reason why the American didn't get back on the train but whatever it was I believe that McKern intended at that stage to steal the money from him and arranged with his friend to probably kidnap Joe when he went to collect it, kill him and he'd share the money between them. Remember," the Inspector went on. "McKern couldn't do much with that arm so he had to have help."

The sergeant, anxious to show that he was following his hypothesis added, "And then the following week Cope had an Army vehicle to take some supplies to Glasgow and used it on their return to Carlisle to carry the body, which they dumped in the Clyde at Bothwell."

Alright so far, sergeant?"

"Can't find fault with that yet, sir."

"With the message you've just received it appears that Cope had his share hidden away and the one-hundred pound note we found in McKern's flat confirms that he must have had his share of the money there. Whatever they, or even Cope on his own, had planned, it was held up because of McKern's operation on his arm. But as soon as he came out of hospital Cope suddenly took it into his head to take Andy's share by murdering him, pick up his share of the loot and then disappear."

"But we rumbled him and he was caught when he returned to the camp," the sergeant concluded. "But where did all that money come from in the first place sir? Who did he plan to meet at Glasgow I wonder? £34,000 is a hell of a lot of money.

"We'll never know, unless you'd begin a separate investigation when I've taken my pension, but remember the only people who could have told you are now all dead!"

Chief Inspector Alistair McIntosh rose from his chair and, looking very pleased with himself. "I think I'd better go and see the Chief now and you can start on the report, sergeant."

"Er, just before you go, Chief Inspector..." Sergeant Baillie rarely addressed Alistair as formally as that and he stopped dead in his tracks. It was almost as though he was being questioned about a serious error of judgement he had made.

"What is it, Baillie?"
"Where did Hartwell say he got that diamond?"
Alistair suddenly realised that when he had begun to see the conclusion of this, his last case, he'd forgotten to ask the sailor about it. "Oh that!" the inspector was searching to find a plausible excuse. "Oh that!" he repeated, "Does it really matter? It can't be anything to do with the case, and I can't afford to start on another enquiry. I'm retiring, sergeant, had you forgotten?"

PART TWO

CHAPTER THIRTY-ONE

Alistair McIntosh had spent nearly all his life as a policeman but now being retired he was bored.
He joined the City of Glasgow Police in 1910 aged eighteen and his service had been continuous. A number of his colleagues had volunteered to join the army as soon as war was declared in 1914, but he was saddened to learn that very soon many of them would never come back. When the Chief Constable ordered that no more police should enlist as it was depleting the Force, Alistair was obliged to conform and join in with the other officers who were prevented from doing what their colleagues had done. To soften the blow, the ones remaining were told that they would be needed for other equally important duties. That gave them some sort of a feeling of importance after missing out on fighting the Germans and defending their country in time of war, which appeared at first to be the right thing to do.
Soon after peace was declared in 1918, he was transferred to Paisley, the town where he was born, and married a girl some ten years younger than himself, but it didn't quite work out. After his divorce he married his present wife, Judy, and his career took off, reaching the rank of Detective Chief Inspector in the 1940s.
He was sitting in an easy chair reading the Glasgow Herald, scanning the pages for every story that dealt with the crimes in the city. There were one or two reports of soldiers using violence against wives who had been unfaithful while they had been away. The soldiers had also sought out the men who had been guilty of having the affairs and beaten them up rather badly.
The magistrates seemed to be dealing only with the severest cases where people had to have treatment from the injuries they had received. Alistair had been told that his old colleagues had deliberately turned a blind eye to many of the lesser cases.

In spite of his boredom, he was reluctant to start on any of the household jobs he had promised his wife that he would do after he had left the Force.
Their semi-detached house, built in the 1920s, was in a bad state of repair. Although it had missed any serious damage during the bombing in the 1940s, there were many small items needing attention, and the woodwork outside certainly required a coat or two of paint. There was no one available to do any of those jobs during the war years, but now he was ready with an excuse each time Judy suggested that he might start on some of them. He had often promised her that he would try to do the repairs and redecorate the living room as soon as he retired. The drab, heavily patterned wallpaper had been on the walls since the day they moved in soon after the house was built, but Alistair had no desire to redecorate for the moment. During the summer months he had used what time he had looking after his garden.
Over the years some of the younger constables had helped him with most of the rough and heavy work and, as with others in the neighbourhood, the garden had supplied them with a good crop of vegetables throughout the war.
Judy had accepted the inevitability of Alistair's delayed retirement, but she was disappointed when she discovered that he had little inclination to do anything else but sit and read the newspaper and sleep. She was also beginning to feel that the light had gone out of her life as well. They had had plans before the war to do many things when Alistair retired but the last five years had taken its toll on both of them.
Judy had had an active life when they lived in Paisley. She had worked for the ship building company of Fleming and Ferguson as a young clerk and had been lucky enough to have kept her job during the years of national depression in the early 1930s. She always boasted that she almost ran the office and certainly played an important role in teaching the young girls all the clerical work that was required to enable the company to run smoothly.
She left the firm in 1936 when Alistair had been promoted to Inspector, and they then moved to the house in Glasgow in which

they now lived. Her organising ability made it somewhat natural for her to be a prominent member of the WVS and she had had some harrowing experiences around the area of the docks during the bombing of Glasgow in the early 1940s. With their busy lives they never seemed to have time to bring up a family and regretted later that they never had any children.
Judy made two coffees and took them into the living room where Alistair was sitting.
"Why don't you stop reading about crime and forget the whole thing? You're not a Chief Inspector now, only plain Alistair McIntosh. Turn to the sports pages or something. It'll only make you more depressed reading about cases that you're not able to deal with."
"I suppose you're right Judy, but it's not easy for me to ignore what has been my whole life."
"But now we have a new life, so why don't we enjoy ourselves and get off for a week or two, away from this place and have a holiday in Oban perhaps, or go to Fort William to visit your sister?"
Alistair thrust his newspaper down onto his lap, showing the white of his knuckles as his hands gripped the pages. "Oh, spare me that Judy. I'd rather go to Inverness on the opposite coast far away from her!"
His sister had never forgiven him from the day when Alistair left his first wife and married Judy. He had always avoided any discussion with her in regard to the reasons, and had never had any intentions of doing so, especially as he had now been happily married to his second wife for over fifteen years.
His first wife, Mary, had never accepted that his job entailed very unsociable hours and that inevitably led to arguments. She was a pretty blonde with blue eyes as big as saucers. Alistair had fallen desperately in love with her and had been aware that if he did not win her over someone else would beat him to it. But when the passion wore off she became discontented with being just the wife of a policeman. She preferred to go to dances and have a good

time rather than wait in to cook his meal when he came home at unexpected times. He became very unhappy until he met Judy.
Judy had a completely different outlook on life. Although she was quite plain with short dark hair framing her somewhat serious-looking face, Alistair found her to be very compassionate. They liked the same things and she was interested in what he did.
Mary had found out that he was seeing a lot of this other woman, but preferred to ignore it as it gave her an excuse for more freedom and to do what she wanted. Inevitably the marriage became sour and he eventually left Mary to go and live with Judy. Divorce followed, and Mary went away from the area. Later Alistair and Judy were married at Paisley registry Office, and since then have had a very happy life together.

"Well then, come on Alistair, what do you want to do about it? Where shall we go?" Judy stood patiently waiting for an answer.
Alistair returned his newspaper back to its original position and glanced over the page he had been reading. "I'm not making any decisions at this very moment. I'll need to think it out carefully."
"You mean as you used to do when you solved a crime?" Judy said sarcastically. "My motives are to get you away from here and avoid visits from your past colleagues, especially that Sergeant Baillie."
Alistair didn't answer. He knew his wife was right but was loath to admit it. He had been used to making all the decisions and he was finding it difficult to accept that someone else was questioning his motives and trying to make up his mind for him. Judy was aware of this and knew that she would not get an answer from him until he was ready. She put the cup down on the small table next to him. "Don't forget to drink your coffee," she reminded him sharply.

Alistair was looking at the newspaper but he was not reading it. His mind was elsewhere. His wife had mentioned Sergeant Baillie and although he had never asked, he often wondered whether all the loose ends of his last case had been tied up. It had been concluded to his satisfaction but there was still a mystery about

where a very large amount of money had originated. Still more intriguing was how a young Naval rating, a mechanic in the Fleet Air Arm, had in his possession a very expensive diamond and then sold it for a large amount of money to a dealer he had met in a Glasgow hotel. It just didn't make sense.
Then he found that the girl, who had spent a couple of nights with the sailor in the hotel pretending to be his wife, was also acquainted with the American soldier who had been murdered. In addition, did she also know the Scottish soldier who had been killed? he wondered.. These were all questions that had been left unresolved but there was no evidence to prove that either she, or her boy friend was connected to the murders.

Thinking about this reminded him of another case, which had also been left unsolved just after he became a sergeant in Paisley in 1931. That case had never been satisfactorily concluded and the murderer, if there had been one, had never been discovered. As an ordinary police constable, he had not been involved in any of the investigations and, in fact, it had been Judy who had first told him about the missing person at the time, but unlike these latest murders, the body was never found.

CHAPTER THIRTY-TWO

Alistair folded up the newspaper very carefully as his mind went back to what had happened. Everyone had been baffled as to why Ian McBride, the gardener from the Poor House in Craw Road, had mysteriously disappeared.

Surely the case was too cold for it to be re-opened but if he could get hold of the papers, perhaps it would give him just the thing he was looking for to make life more interesting again. He had been glad to leave the force but now with no pressure on him to try to solve the mystery, it would be something for him to do. However, he knew that after all this time there would be very little hope of discovering what had happened to Ian McBride.

When Judy came to remind him to drink his coffee, Alistair casually remarked, "I think it would be nice to visit some of our old friends in Paisley who we haven't seen for a while. You know I spent most of my early years there and I've never really had the opportunity to go back."

Judy could not believe what he was saying. "You've always said that you didn't want to go back to that god-forsaken place! What on earth has made you want to go back there now after all this time? We haven't got any real friends left in Paisley, and, apart from perhaps Annie McBride, there's no one else I'd want to visit. If I remember correctly, you made more enemies than friends as a policeman, and that included most of your school chums!" she reminded him, as she went back into the kitchen

Alistair turned his head towards her and raised his voice so that she could hear what else he had to say.

"I did make an official visit to the station on a couple of occasions if you remember, and I just thought it would be nice to go back. It would be a nostalgic journey to the areas where I used to patrol the streets."

Alistair heard a grunting noise coming from the kitchen.

"You will also remember," he went on, "that awful tragedy at the Glen cinema all those years ago. Well, I've been thinking, while I was there, I could also pay a visit to the Abbey and the two

cemeteries where many of those poor children were buried after losing their lives."
Judy recalled how badly he had been affected by that event when he had returned home at the end of that terrible day: his haunted look, and his face devoid of any colour. He had been unable to speak about it for a long time afterwards.
She remembered when, together with other officers, he had gone to every funeral of the sixty-nine children who had lost their lives in the fire at the cinema. For months afterwards he had nightmares reliving the tragic event, imagining hearing the screams of those young children as firemen broke windows to try and rescue them. When they eventually managed to open the locked door of the building, he told her that the horrifying sight of a heaped mass of children, moaning and crying in agony would never be able to leave his mind. He had always said that he wished he could have done more to save some of those young bairns.
Judy could tell what he was thinking about and she remained silent. Perhaps to visit the Abbey would help him to come to terms with the tragedy and put his mind to rest after all this time. She looked towards him and saw that his eyes were full of tears, some trickling down his cheeks. She walked over to him and put a gentle arm round his shoulder, her head tilted and resting on his.
"Perhaps it would be nice for you to have that nostalgic visit but, Alistair dear, you mustn’t keep blaming yourself for not being able to do more at the time."
"I know," Alistair blew his nose hard into his handkerchief after drying his eyes.
"I realise that it’s been almost sixteen years since it happened and some of the older boys must have served their country in this last war and most likely seen, or experienced, worse tragedies that those, but I’d still like to go and visit the place for the last time."
Judy could see that he had made up his mind to have that last visit, but was completely unaware that he also had an ulterior motive for going back, which was really nothing to do with that particular event. The tragedy he was equally concerned with was that of the missing gardener. He had never understood why the detective,

Inspector Bob Fairbrother, had given up so easily. Everyone knew that Ian McBride enjoyed a wee dram - or two. The conclusion was reached was that he had probably lost his balance while walking too near the river Cart and had fallen in. If that had been the case, why was a body never found? It was normal for bodies to float back to the surface as happened in a number of cases, but this one never did. Most likely, the reason was that perhaps it was not in the river in the first place.

Alistair remembered that at the time there had been a lot of whispering going on at the station but no one, from the Chief Superintendent downwards, seemed to bother very much about what had happened to him. Could there have been something that he was never told about? Now that he had so much more experience in detective work, he would look forward to reopening the case into Ian McBride's disappearance. Perhaps there was something important that had been overlooked, but the first thing he would have to find out was whether Ian McBride's body had ever been found.

"And now you have a cold cup of coffee," his wife exclaimed as she came to take his cup away. "Shall I make you another?"

"Tomorrow is Friday, so if you've nothing planned, perhaps we could go tomorrow for the weekend."

Although he had not said where, Judy guessed that he was talking about going to Paisley. She knew instinctively he had not meant Oban. "You can if you really want to. But do you mind if I don't come with you? What could I possibly do while you are having your nostalgic journey? You'll no doubt want to call in the station to see if any of your old colleagues are still there and I would only be in the way. So off you go and enjoy yourself for a day or two, and make sure you wrap up. I remember Paisley was always cold in October."

Judy suddenly remembered that he had mentioned wanting to visit the Abbey cemetery and wishing that she had chosen a more appropriate word than 'enjoy', but Alistair appeared not to have heard her. He was contemplating what he was going to do when he got his hands on the report at the Police Station.

CHAPTER THIRTY-THREE

Next morning he set out early, promising himself that he would use all his skill and experience to be able to discover why and how Ian McBride had disappeared.
He pulled into the police station yard, straightened his tie and fastened the buttons on his double- breasted suit before entering the station.
"What can we do for you sir?" the young policeman asked Alistair as he approached the desk.
The sergeant behind him turned and his face lit up. "Detective Inspector Alistair McIntosh. So good to see you. How are you enjoying your retirement?
"Not Detective Inspector or even Chief Inspector, George. It's just plain Alistair McIntosh now, so you can forget the ranks."
The sergeant reached over to take Alistair's hand. "You look remarkably well Alistair. What are you doing with yourself now you have plenty of time on your hands?" He turned to look at the young policeman who looked embarrassed at not having known who it was that had walked unannounced into the station.
"This gentleman is one of the longest serving policemen you're ever likely to meet," the sergeant explained to the bewildered young man. "He started his career here as a young copper before the war, and I mean the first one, not the one that has just ended, made up to sergeant in, was it 1932 Alistair? And then he went to Glasgow as a Detective Inspector. One of the quickest promotions from sergeant to inspector in the force, and then when he was due to retire, made him Chief Inspector until the end of the war 'cos they couldn't afford to let him go. Isn't that right Alistair?"
Alistair nodded, smiling broadly as his old colleague outlined a catalogue of his service.
"Well, something like that, but the war played an important part as you well know, but how yer doing George? Haven't seen you for, how many years is it now?"
"Does it matter? I'll be taking my pension soon to make way for all these youngsters coming into the Force."

George Craythorn had been made sergeant when Alistair had been promoted in 1936 and had remained at Paisley ever since. They both could have written a book about their joint experiences. George sensed that Alistair's visit was not just a social call.
"I can't imagine that you just came here to say hello to me. Have you called in to see our new Chief Inspector? He only came to us last month."
There was something in George's tone of voice that sounded a little disrespectful for his new chief, but it was an excuse that Alistair was looking for. "How did you guess George? Is he available?"
George gave Alistair a wink as he walked toward the door along the corridor. "I'll go and see."
When George returned, he again winked at Alistair. "I told him that an old colleague of mine who has just retired after a long and distinguished career in the force had asked to see you. He told me to tell you to go straight in."
A very smartly dressed officer met Alistair as he entered his office. He looked remarkably young; not more than in his early forties. His handshake was limp and his palm felt clammy. When he spoke, Alistair could tell instantly that his accent was not a local one, more of an educated voice: probably from Edinburgh.
"I understand from my sergeant that you began your police career here at this station, er, Mr McIntosh. Is this a visit to see where it all began?"
Alistair felt a little uncomfortable with the formal and less friendly greeting, the newly appointed officer obviously assuming that he was on a nostalgic visit so he just briefly nodded, but certainly didn't enjoy being referred to as plain Mr McIntosh. He thought it less than respectful.
"Please sit down and we can have a little chat." He introduced himself as Chief Inspector Donald Campbell, briefly glancing at his watch as he sat down. Alistair seated himself in the only other chair in the room on the opposite side of his desk. He felt as if he was about to be interviewed. Perhaps he had to get used to the idea of not being in charge. He thought that he would explain

what he had come about and get it over with as quickly as possible.
"Sergeant Craythorn has no doubt just told you that I retired from the force last May and I thought that I'd just like to come back here on a nostalgic visit." He didn't feel inclined to tell him about the other reason he was visiting Paisley so he thought he would come straight to the point.
"However, there is something I would like to know and I believe that you might be able to help me." He rested his arms on the side of the chair and shuffled a little in his seat.
"About sixteen years ago, a couple of years or so before I was promoted to sergeant, there was a mystery about a missing person. I wasn't really involved as it was investigated by the then Detective Inspector and other police officers and I was just a constable, but I knew the missing man Ian McBride very well, and his family, but the case was never satisfactorily concluded, mainly because his body was never found. For some reason, everyone felt that he disappeared somewhere in this area but no one appeared to investigate the reason for his disappearance. There was talk about his private life but I always believed that it was hushed up for one reason or another. When I became a detective inspector in Glasgow, I made myself a promise that when I retired and if it was possible, I would go through the papers of the case just to satisfy myself that no stone had been left unturned, and maybe discover what really happened to Ian McBride."
There was a long pause as the Chief Inspector stared at his visitor. He then placed his arms on the desk and leaned over towards Alistair. "Now before you go on, you know as well as I, that what you are suggesting is impossible. Firstly, and most importantly, you are no longer on the force, and therefore, not entitled to look at any of the papers of any case investigated here, whether solved or not. Secondly, if I allowed you to see the papers, even if they are still here, I would be in trouble and probably lose my job."
Unusually for Alistair, he had not expected this. His hands began to tighten on the arms of the chair. He wanted to argue and tell this jumped-up inexperienced officer just what he thought He

immediately lost all respect for him, feeling that his remarks were a sort of reprimand and it was obvious that he was not even going to discuss his request. When he had previously been in a similar situation he had always found it best to go on to the attack.
"Well, I'm sorry I asked you for this information and know now that I shouldn't have troubled you. With my experience I ought to have realised that you would refuse. As a retired Detective Chief Inspector, I ought to have gone straight to the Chief Constable."
Alistair moved his chair a little and raised himself up indicating that he was about to leave.
Chief Inspector Donald Campbell shuffled uneasily in his chair. He may have been inexperienced but he was no fool. First he had not been told by his sergeant that Alistair had been a Chief Inspector and, furthermore, now he had learned who his visitor was, he could see what the implications might be when the Chief Constable learned that he had refused to help one of his senior and most experienced Detective Chief Inspectors, whom he probably knew and respected, even if he had recently retired.
"Now just wait a second, er Alistair," he said in a much more friendly tone. "You don't mind if I call you Alistair?"
Alistair nodded as he sat back in his chair, satisfied that his ruse had worked.
"We'll just see first if there are any papers about the case still in the files. I'll get my sergeant to step in, and ask him what he knows."
The answer to the Inspector's question was answered almost immediately. George Craythorn said he remembered being told about three or four years after the disappearance of Ian McBride, that the papers could be destroyed, namely, because the evidence clearly pointed to his having fallen in the river and his body probably being washed out to sea with the tide.
"Do you remember who told you to get rid of the papers, sergeant?"
"Certainly. It was Detective Inspector Fairbrother. He told me that in his opinion there was no point in keeping them."

Alistair thought that Inspector Donald Campbell looked relieved and quite pleased at the sergeant's revelations. "Thank you, sergeant. That is all."
The Chief Inspector waited for his door to close before rising from his chair, his face now relaxed and wearing an expression of relief at the outcome. He was pleased that the case was dead and gone as far as his own responsibility was concerned.
"I'm sorry, Chief Inspector, we are unable to help you. We naturally might have been able to discuss it further if we had anything to go on, but you can see that we haven't, so my advice is to let the matter drop and go and enjoy your well earned retirement."
He moved towards the door with his hand outstretched and a broad grin on his face. Alistair shook the hand that still seemed to him like a piece of wet fish.
"What was all that about?" the sergeant asked as Alistair left the Chief's office.
"Well you must remember all the mystery about the disappearance of Ian McBride? We were both young constables when all that happened. I take it that his body was never recovered from the river - that is if it was ever there in the first place," Alistair added as an afterthought.
"You're right, Alistair. It never did turn up and the detective who did the investigations never mentioned it to anybody afterwards as I recall. But I do remember one of our new lads asking him about it a year or so afterwards - I don't remember which one it was now, but I can still see Bob Fairbrother shrugging his shoulders and walking away, leaving the youngster feeling a bit dropped on, and thinking that perhaps that he shouldn't have asked. Why have you suddenly become interested after all this time?"
"Well, George, I've often thought about it. I knew Ian's wife very well and always felt sorry for his young lad, David, losing his dad in that way with no explanation as to what actually happened. His son was only a wee bairn at the time, five or six I believe. I saw him once when I came here on a brief visit during the war and he looked rather smart in his PAMS uniform. You will remember, of

course, those young lads that were enrolled in the Police Auxiliary Messenger Service who had the thankless job of delivering the telegrams about sons and husbands missing, or killed.
"That young lad knew who I was, and asked me in a very quiet voice, so that nobody else could hear, whether I ever knew anything about his dad’s disappearance. I think it was then that I thought perhaps one day I might ask around to try and establish that nothing had been overlooked in the enquiry at the time."
George thought that Alistair would be wasting his time."But no one could discover what happened to Ian at the time. What do’yer hope to achieve by further investigations?"
"I don’t know, George, but now I’ve got a lot more experience in this sort of thing, and, who knows, perhaps someone will talk more freely to me than they were prepared to do to others after Ian's disappearance."
George took him by the hand as he prepared to leave. It was a firm grip and just the opposite to the Inspector’s floppy handshake. "Well, best of luck, Alistair, but don’t be too disappointed if it all comes to nothing."
"I won’t, George, but I have never heard of someone destroying the papers of a case that hadn't been finalised, which seems to me a little more than unusual. I intend to give it some more thought and decide whether or not to come back. I have decided now to go back home today as I don’t want to get mixed up with the crowds for St Mirren’s home match tomorrow."

Alistair eventually left the police station somewhat disappointed. He had thought when he arrived that he would have some of the papers giving him the background of the case to take home and study, but now he left with nothing to go on. He walked on for a while without realising in which direction, but noticed that he was close to Lochfyeld Primary School. His thoughts went back to the cinema disaster and what had happened to some of the small children who were pupils at that school at the time of the tragedy. He suddenly remembered that the other reason for his visit to his old town was to visit the cemetery and that was where he must now go.

He made his way to the Abbey where the memorial service had taken place in the week following the disaster and sat for a while at the back of the church in quiet thought, remembering all those children who had lost their lives in the cinema on 30 December 1930. It was something he had wished to do for a very long time and now without the pressure of work he had a moment to reflect on what had been the saddest day of his life.

He made a brief visit to some of the graves at Woodside Cemetery before deciding to go straight home, but disappointed at not having achieved what he had set out to do. With nothing to go on as far as Ian McBride was concerned, he wondered whether he had been wasting his time looking for something that had never existed. If there had been anything sinister about the disappearance of the Poor House gardener, surely the enquiries made at the time would have revealed them.

He drove home to Glasgow in his old black Hillman with a heavy heart, contemplating that perhaps there would be no point in further investigations after all into Ian McBride's disappearance.

CHAPTER THIRTY-FOUR

Judy was surprised to see her husband return; "I thought you would be in Paisley for at least another day. Why have you come back so soon?"
Alistair explained what had happened and told her that he considered that it would be too difficult to do anything further in the disappearance of Ian McBride and in any case, it had not been possible to get any help from the police.
Alistair looked so forlorn that Judy felt sorry that his journey had been for nothing. She knew that he had always been convinced that he would be able to do something and found it difficult to understand what had made him give up so easily.
She had had a visit from Sergeant Baillie that morning asking to see her husband. She had promised herself that she would not tell Alistair because she guessed from the sergeant's attitude that it was something to do with a previous case and she did not want him to get involved again. She had also reminded the sergeant that Alistair was retired and if it was about when he was working, then unless it was really urgent perhaps he might give it to the others to deal with. Although he looked a trifle embarrassed as he left, he had said that he was sure that his old boss would be interested to know what he had to tell him but it was not really that urgent.
Judy waited until her husband had sat down before she mentioned his old sergeant's visit.
"I suppose that I'd better tell you that that Sergeant Baillie came this morning and said that he wanted to see you about something."
Alistair suddenly brightened up. "Did he say what it was about?"
"I'm afraid that I didn't let him, but I did remind him that you have retired and he shouldn't be worrying you about things now."
Alistair got up from where he had been sitting. "I think I'll go and see him," he announced with fresh enthusiasm.
"Oh no you don't. You've done enough for one day and you'll sit there and relax. Knowing how you used to work I bet you haven't eaten much since you left here this morning."

Alistair immediately realised that what she had said was true. He had been so absorbed in what he had been doing in Paisley that he had not thought about food. The young policeman at the station had made him a cup of coffee on George's instructions, but apart from that and a couple of digestive biscuits he had not had anything else to eat all day.
"Stay where you are and I'll get you a glass of scotch and then we'll have a nice meal. You've got to learn to put all this nonsense of police work behind you."
Although he was impatient to find out the reason that Baillie wanted to see him, Alistair felt relieved that his wife had stopped him from going out. He felt tired after his day's outing, no doubt bitterly disappointed at the outcome at the police station and then later emotionally drained following his visit to the Abbey. He had been in charge for most of his career and not used to being told what to do but he suddenly felt surprisingly content to let his wife take over at least on this one occasion.
The day had not turned out as he had first hoped and his ulcer always seemed to play him up whenever he felt any stress. Furthermore, he could not get out of his mind the look of self-gratification on the face of that young inspector at Paisley after he had discovered that there was nothing for Alistair to do in the case he had inquired about, so he sat back in his favourite armchair and listened to some dance music on the wireless as he relaxed with the glass of scotch that his wife had given him.
After a good night's sleep he woke early next morning feeling fully refreshed. He got out of bed without waking his wife and went downstairs to make himself an early breakfast. First he laid the fire in the living room and lit it then went back into the kitchen. He sprinkled some porridge oats straight from the packet into a small saucepan of boiling water, added a pinch of salt and turned the gas down to simmer.
While waiting for the porridge to cook and thicken, giving it a stir now and again so that it wouldn't burn, he cut himself a thick slice of bread from a new cottage loaf that Judy had made and spread it carefully with a meagre amount of butter bearing in mind that it

was still on ration, conscious that the small amount in the dish had to last the week. He spread a generous amount of Judy's homemade marmalade on to his bread and ate this after his dish of porridge. Feeling very satisfied with what he considered to be an excellent breakfast he made a pot of tea and took a cup up to his wife.

She opened her eyes and glanced at the clock. It was still only twenty minutes to eight "You're up early, and fully dressed too. Where do you think you are going at this time in the morning?"

"At this precise moment, I'm going to fetch a paper. I've already had my breakfast and then I'm taking your advice and going to sit down all morning with the 'Scotsman', listen to the wireless and relax."

It was precisely 3 o'clock when Sergeant Baillie came to the house. He had noticed Alistair's car parked outside when he passed by so guessed that he would be at home.

Judy had seen him coming when she looked out of the window and it crossed her mind to say that her husband was asleep or some other excuse to prevent him from being disturbed but she opened the door as soon as he rang and reluctantly invited him in and went back into the kitchen.

"Robert, how good to see you." It was the first time that Sergeant Baillie could ever remember being addressed by his Christian name by his old boss. "Judy told me that you came to see me yesterday but I was paying a visit to Paisley. What's new?" Alistair waved his hand to indicate for him to sit down opposite him.

Sitting in an easy chair facing his Inspector and being called "Robert" gave Baillie an unusual feeling of being totally relaxed. It was in complete contrast to the years of their official meetings sitting on hard chairs in the police station and being ordered to do things. Now he suddenly felt even perhaps a little more important than the man opposite especially as he had in his possession information about Alistair's last case that had been left unsolved.

CHAPTER THIRTY-FIVE

Alistair could hardly wait for his old sergeant to tell him the latest news, guessing that he'd come to tell what he had discovered further about the money that McKern and Cope had in their possession. He didn't want to sound too eager for Judy's sake so he sat back in his chair apparently appearing to only be vaguely interested. .

Judy walked in. "Cup of tea Robert?"

Alistair looked daggers at his wife. Judy had intervened at the wrong moment

"Er, No thank you Judy. I've only come for a moment. I have to get back."

Alistair fidgeted in his chair and looked hard at his visitor. He stopped himself from saying, Go on then tell me!

Robert Baillie got the message.

"You remember that we wondered where the large amount of money had come from that we found in the soldier's possession. Well, we have discovered some more. By 'we', I mean that the police in the village in Dorset where Miss Harrison was employed as a barmaid in the Cricketer's Arms. When we told them that we had no further interest in her and that we were satisfied that she or her sailor boy friend had no involvement of the murdered G.I., they became suspicious when she left the pub and began spending a lot of money mainly Scottish fivers similar to the ones found on the man who was shot."

"Now that's interesting." Alistair leaned forward in his chair anxious to hear what the Dorset police had discovered. "Tell me more."

"They made discreet enquiries from the landlord at the pub, Cornelius Hill," the sergeant was now consulting his notebook as he spoke, "who thought she had been given some money from an aunt that she went to see in Glasgow."

"We knew nothing about an aunt did we sergeant?" Alistair automatically reverted back to calling him sergeant now that he was speaking about official police business.

It put Robert on his guard and he began to wonder whether he should address the ex-inspector as sir. Instead he just answered, "No! The police did nothing until that Howard Hartwell came to the village on leave and then suddenly married her."
"You're going to tell me that she's pregnant!"
The sergeant looked surprised and frowned. He thought that his old boss was being flippant about what he regarded as an important discovery .
"I don't know about that but they were married at the Registry Office in Weymouth."
"Well, it doesn't surprise me that they got married. It was pretty obvious that they were more than just friends but I suppose it was a bit soon as they hadn't known each other for very long."
"Ah! but the point is that their money was now beginning to flow like water. They bought a gift shop that was up for sale in the village for £350 and they paid cash for it with more of those five pound notes."
"Wait a minute. Do the Dorset police know that Hartwell got hundreds of pounds for that diamond he sold to a jeweller at that hotel? I recall that the hotel cashed the cheque the jeweller gave him which could have accounted for all that money and the girl could have lied about getting the money from her probably non-existent aunt because she didn't want her old boss to know where the money had come from."
Ignoring Alistair's comments, Sergeant Baillie continued, "So that led us to try to find out where the diamond came from and how a sailor could have had such a valuable stone in his possession. Was it his to sell we wondered?."
"Who's 'we'?" Alistair asked, now concerned that a large number of people seemed to be getting involved in tying up the few loose ends he had left. Surely it was not that important to warrant a lot of police work
Again not answering his Inspector Baillie went on, "You will agree that the diamond was always a mystery to us so we thought that if we traced where the money had come from we might find a connection to the diamond."

Alistair thought that somebody was chasing a lost cause here. "Surely we both know that the money probably came from the sale of the diamond so that would tell you nothing."
"Ah! But then the police discovered that the couple had banked over £800 with the Midland Bank in Weymouth before they got married, which takes the total amount to something nearer to fifteen hundred pounds they must have had in their possession.. If there wasn't a generous aunt in existence as the girl claimed, then where did all that extra money come from?"
Alistair said nothing not wishing to make another foolish observation when he had been unaware of the facts. "So, are you telling me that you have now found out?"
The sergeant shuffled in his seat. "Well. No, not really, but we are getting nearer to a solution."
"Have the Dorset police questioned both of them as to where they got that extra money?"
"Of course."
"...And?" Alistair waited patiently, expecting that his sergeant was about to reveal all.
"Howard told them that it was none of their business and in any case he said that it was his own money. No one had reported that they had lost any money or had been robbed of any large amount of cash either in Dorset or Scotland so the police could go no further without more evidence."
"So you're stumped" Alistair said with some gratification. He had expected that Baillie was going to tell him that he had tied up all those loose ends that he had left undone, but it had turned out to be a story about nothing.
"And you are no nearer to finding out about the diamond either?"
"No, 'fraid not. Hartwell just said that Elizabeth had told him that it was given to her by that American and then forgot to take it with her when she left the hotel. The girl confirmed that story when questioned and said that Joe had given her other jewellery, which most turned out to be costume jewellery and was surprised when Howard discovered the diamond to be real."

Alistair shook his head. "Well, no one will be able to ask the American where he got it from now will they? So we'll never know, and that just leaves us to wish the lucky couple a happy marriage."
Alistair sat back with his thoughts concentrating on the attractive girl. He was pleased that nothing had been discovered that would implicate her in the murders that had taken place or of any criminal activity. His attention was drawn to Sergeant Baillie putting his notebook back into his pocket
"Have you always kept your own notes about cases that you've been involved with, Robert?"
"They're just unofficial and I put my own comments side by side with what I know. Why do you ask? I thought that you always knew I did that."
Alistair suddenly became very interested in what the sergeant was saying. He was wondering if any of the police officers at Paisley had kept a similar notebook with their own observations as to what had happened to Ian McBride. It may have been a long time ago but thought perhaps that it might be worth following up. He was still wondering about it when he heard his wife telling him that Robert was leaving.
"Oh, sorry Robert." Alistair rose from his chair, "I was far away thinking about something else. Your notebook has given me an idea about something I'm interested in."
He was unaware of the glare his wife was giving him as she read his thoughts and his old sergeant also didn't miss the inference.
"Just be careful what you get up to sir. Remember that you're retired and should be taking it easy."

CHAPTER THIRTY-SIX

Immediately after Alistair closed the outside door when the sergeant had left, he noticed that his wife was giving him one of her 'knowing' looks.
"I realise what's on your mind Alistair. Will you promise me to let the matter drop about Ian McBride? There's no point in you going on with your investigations. I don't really know what you are trying to achieve. For goodness sake forget it." She turned her back on him before he could answer and went briskly into the kitchen to prepare lunch. She was convinced that she had had the last word on the subject.
Alistair sat down on a chair in front of the bureau, took out a piece of paper from the writing pad and began listing the names of every policeman at Paisley whom he could remember that would have had some knowledge of the enquiries that were made at the time of Ian McBride's disappearance. He was so absorbed in what he was doing that he did not hear his wife re-enter the room and creep up behind him.
"I thought so. You're either obsessed with this business or you're off your head and I can't decide which." She had her fists clenched and her face was flushed revealing how angry she was feeling. "It's all a complete waste of time and giving me no consideration whatsoever. I can't imagine what's come over you."
Alistair put down his pen and turned to face her. "Judy, my love, just allow me to get this business of Ian McBride out of my system and then I will not discuss or think about any other case ever again. I promise you that when it's all over, I'll take you on a long holiday to wherever you want to go. OK?"
Judy could see that it was no use arguing with him. He had made up his mind and she knew him too well to discuss the matter further.
"Will you write down what you just said?"
"Write what down?"

"Write down that you will take me on a long holiday when you've done what you have to do and won't ever discuss or deal with police work afterwards."
Alistair was trapped and it was entirely his own making but he thought that perhaps she was right to demand that he should keep his promise to her. He had no other case in mind anyway, so he immediately agreed to her request.
"I promise." he said with sincerity and with his hand over his heart.
"Then get writing Alistair McIntosh."

CHAPTER THIRTY-SEVEN

After contemplating his course of action over the weekend, Alistair made his first call to the Paisley Police Station at about 11am on Monday to see George Craythorn. The sergeant was just about to go on a call. A report had been received about a disturbance at a house in Gilmour Street, which required his attention.
"Leave your car here Alistair and come with me. We can talk on the way."
Whatever his old friend was about to encounter, Alistair felt secure sitting in the passenger seat next to the sergeant.
George was a well-built man who obviously kept himself fit. He was also an inch or two over six feet in height and if there was going to be any trouble Alistair felt confident that George would be able to handle it.
"Well I can guess why you've come back. Still wanting to pursue your enquiries in regard to Ian McBride I expect"
"You've guessed it. I came to you first because I think you will know where I can get hold of the people whose names I have on my list."
"Right. We're nearly there. I'll go through them with you after I've dealt with this."
The car pulled up and even before George had switched off the engine the noise of shouting and swearing could be heard coming from the house where it had been reported that there had been a disturbance..
"You wait here. I'll soon deal with this."
As he got out of the car, women standing on either on side of the gate in their pinnies with arms folded began telling him what had been going on. George put his hand up to silence them without success. Walking swiftly to the door he went straight inside the house without knocking. Alistair then heard a loud bellowing man's voice and the high-pitched screech of a woman's as he listened to all the three voices seemingly talking together. Soon after that the shouting stopped until eventually all went quiet.

After a while, George then appeared in the doorway looking quite pleased with himself.
Alistair guessed that after quietening the occupants down he had no doubt listened to their arguments before giving them a lecture and probably a final warning. As he walked away from the now quiet house, all the women spectators stopped talking as they looked at the police sergeant, waiting to hear what he had to say.
Walking past them he said in a quiet voice, "You can all go back to your homes now. The war's over!"
As he approached the car, a soldier in a kilt came out of the door and, without pausing or glancing at anyone, marched quickly down the street. Alistair noticed his clenched fists and his angry-looking red face.
George chuckled as he sat down and closed the car door." That wasn't as bad as it sounded."
"Why? What happened?" Alistair was amused at the way that George had dealt with the situation so quickly and with obvious success.
Pointing to the kilted Highlander, George explained, "He's just come home and heard rumours that his wife had been entertaining other soldiers while he'd been away. He threatened to kill her. He told me that coming home to a bitch of a wife caused him to lose his bloody temper as he put it.
She had tried to tell him that only on one occasion had she invited two Polish soldiers back to the house for a coffee - blokes she felt sorry for when she worked in the railway cafe. The old tongues got going and the troublemakers put two and two together and made ten. When she tried to explain that there was no harm in what she's done, he didn't believe her and accused her of having it off with them while he was away fighting."
"And do yer think she did?"
"She did what?"
"Have an affair or do you think she was telling the truth?"
"I don't know but I told him that if he did kill her he'd be hanged for it. He said that he hadn't thought about that as he flew into a rage as soon as he got in, thrown some dishes at her in his temper

which made a loud noise as they crashed against the wall,. Luckily they missed her, so hearing the noise and fearing for his wife's life some of the neighbours rang the police station. I managed to calm him down and now I expect he's going to the pub to get drunk. He smelt of booze when I went in. He'll come to his senses when he's sobered up."
"So where we going now?" Alistair was concerned that George had either forgotten what he wanted him to do or that he had to get back to the station immediately.
"I'm moving away from here and I'll park just round the corner and then try to help you with whatever information you need. As soon as the car was stationary he looked at his old friend and smiled. "Right, then, fire away."
Alistair took out the list he had made of people who might be able to help and that he wanted to talk to. After studying the paper for a few seconds George told him "I think I know where you can find all of them except two. Charlie Dimmick joined up and was killed soon after D. Day - you obviously didn't know that and Harry Smith died last year after a heart attack. He had only retired the year before, but there's one name that sticks out, Sergeant John McCloud. Don't you remember? He was the other detective on the case when Ian McBride disappeared."
"I did remember that but something funny went on at the time. Wasn't he surprised to be taken off the case to investigate something else?"
"There was a rumour that Detective Inspector Fairbrother wanted him off the case. I believe it was said at the time that it didn't need two of them to find out the reason why McBride had disappeared. Anyway Fairbrother soon reached the conclusion that he had fallen into the river full of whisky!"
"What, the river or him?"
George chuckled. "Him, you damn fool. Do you want to go and see John McCloud first? I think that would be your best bet. He only retired a few months ago."
"I think you'd better take me back to the station first and then I can pick up my own car."

"I was going to do that anyway" George had already started the car engine and was heading on the way back.
"He lives at Camp Hill not far from the school. I'll give you the house number when we stop and the rest of the addresses.
The mention of Camp Hill School was another reminder of where some of the children came from on that awful day in December all those years ago. He sat very quietly for a while his thoughts elsewhere.
"Did you hear me Alistair? You know where that is don't you?"
"Yes, I know where that is George. Will I ever forget it?"
George guessed immediately what Alistair was referring to and that he had reminded him of it by mentioning the school.
"I think that you ought to get something to eat before you start. In any case, it would be best to see John McCloud after he's had his dinner. There's a nice little cafe in the High Street near to Macintyre Place where you can get something to eat. Everyone works better on a full stomach."
Alistair didn't want to argue with his sergeant friend but he had always found that he was at his best when he was hungry.

CHAPTER THIRTY-EIGHT

The car pulled up next to Alistair's and, as they both shook hands, George wished him all the best and hoped that he would succeed in what he was setting out to try and achieve.
Alistair found the cafe that had been recommended and a young girl waitress approached pad in hand. He noticed that she was very young, not more that fifteen or sixteen. She had a full head of ginger hair and her pretty face was completely covered in freckles. He was not to know that only a few months earlier the same girl had served the young sailor Howard Hartwell and his girl friend Miss Harrison, the two people who had been at the centre of his enquiry in his investigation of the two murders.
"What do'yer like?" The young waitress waited for him to scan the short menu.
"Oh, I'll just have a couple of fish paste sandwiches and a pot of tea thank you."
She brought them to him nicely presented with lettuce and a tomato, which made them look very appetizing.
Being refreshed he made his way to Camp Hill and scanned the houses for the number he had been given hoping that when he got there John McCloud would be in.
John opened the door in answer to Alistair's knocking.
"Good God! Alistair McIntosh! What on earth are you doing here? Come in for goodness sake. Well I never! You'll never guess who just walked in Betty," he shouted as he shut the door.
John's wife appeared and stared at their visitor. "Alistair," she went straight to him and offered her cheek to him for a kiss. "You would call while I'm washing up and see me in my apron."
"And why isn't that lazy husband of yours doing the drying?" Alistair remarked pointing towards him.
"I was doing more important things like reading the paper," John retorted. "Come sit yourself down and tell me all your news. You've retired I heard."

"I have. And I'm enjoying every minute. No, that's a lie," he added quickly. "Judy keeps on to me to wind down take her on holiday and to forget all about my police life."
"And can't you?"
"Well to tell you the truth John, there's one thing that I feel I must do before I give everything up altogether."
Betty walked in at that point carrying a tray with three cups of tea and a plate of digestive biscuits.
"How's Judy? Is she enjoying you being at home all day or are you nearly always in the way like my John?"
"Don't believe her Alistair. She keeps me busy most of the time. I've never been so domesticated before in my whole life."
"That is when I can pull him away from his newspaper and the garden."
John ignored his wife's remarks and was thinking about what Alistair had said before Betty brought in the tea.
"Alistair was about to tell me that he has something to do. Is it important?"
Alistair paused for a moment wondering what was the best way to find out if John knew anything. There was a pregnant silence except for the ticking of the clock on the mantelpiece, which seemed at that moment to be excessively loud.
"I wanted to find...no, that's not quite right. I mean that I have always thought about what might have happened to Ian McBride, you remember John, the gardener who disappeared."
"Of course I remember him. You recall that I..."
Alistair interrupted him before he could finish his sentence. "Did they ever find a body?"
"No and I don't think they ever would at the time."
"Why do'ya say that? There must be a reason."
John finished his cup of tea before answering Alistair's question. Carefully, he placed the empty cup on the saucer and put it down on the table close to his chair. He looked straight at his visitor for a moment as if trying to decide how much he should tell him. Alistair thought that what he was about to hear would be a revelation and possibly just what he wanted to know.

"I know that you and your wife were friends and no doubt always regarded Ian as an innocent, quiet, good upright citizen who could do no wrong as far as you were concerned. Things were kept very quiet at the time and for a very good reason. What I'm going to tell you about him might, no, will, come as a shock to you."
"Well I know that he liked a drink and that he sometimes had a little more than was good for him but that didn't make him a bad character."
"Well, that isn't what I was going to say."
Alistair sensed that John was somewhat reluctant to tell him more and was struggling to find the right way to break the news.
"What I'm sure you don't know is that he was having an affair with P.C.Charlie Dimmick's wife at the time of his disappearance."
"What! Not Ian? I don't believe it. Why on earth didn't I know about it at the time?"
"Because it was deliberately kept quiet for various reasons. I knew that it would be hard for you to swallow but I assure you it was true."
"If that was the case, why weren't there more inquiries and for that matter was Charlie ever a suspect? But more intriguing, why did you say that you didn't think that the body would ever come to light?"
"Now just go steady Alistair. A bit of knowledge could lead to the wrong conclusions. For instance, when I tell you that Bob Fairbrother, who I expect you remember was the detective who investigated the case, and his wife, were great friends of the Dimmicks, you might begin to suspect that someone knew more than was revealed."
"I do remember that it was dealt with very hastily and there was some surprise when it was concluded unusually quickly. How did you find out about Ian and Mrs Dimmick? What was her name now? I forget."
"I'm surprised about that Alistair. Her name was Irene, and you can't tell me that you don't remember her as a very attractive young woman: blonde, nice figure, and in her early twenties at the

time of Ian's disappearance, but did you know that Charlie Dimmick left the force to join the army and was killed in France?"
"George Craythorn told me that and it was he who told me where you lived. I can see now why he told me to come and see you first. I don't suppose he wanted to tell me himself about the affair.. You were on the investigations at the beginning. Why didn't you follow things up?"
"Because, my little innocent Detective Chief Inspector, I was taken off the case as soon as I began to delve into it more deeply after discovering about Charlie's wife's indiscretions. Anyway, it was difficult to follow it up when it was a fellow officer's wife that was involved."
"Who actually took you off the case?"
"I was called into the Chief Superintendent's office and was told that Inspector Bob Fairbrother thought it a waste of manpower for both of us to be investigating Ian McBride's disappearance. The Chief immediately put me on a different case and Bob told me not to breathe a word about the affair, so I kept quiet about what I knew. Bob seemed already to have reached the conclusion that Ian had fallen into the river. I do still have my notebook with the details I wrote at the time."
"Can I see it?" Alistair asked. "Is Charlie's widow still about by the way? And did Annie McBride know about her husband's goings-on?
"I don't think there were serious goings-on as you put it Alistair. Apparently they had only been seeing each other secretly for about a couple of months before Ian's disappearance."
"What I can't believe," Alistair said, "is that I knew Annie very well and she never gave me any indication of being aware of Ian's unfaithfulness, but she must have known about it at the time."
"She probably did but didn't want the world to know about his antics. Anyway I'll go and find that notebook for you to look at. I can't even remember after all this time what I made a note of."
While John was upstairs Betty came back into the room from the kitchen, "Not many knew about that you know. It was kept very quiet at the time."

"But why?"
"No doubt it was to save Charlie Dimmick's face. It must have been really embarrassing for him to find out that his wife was having an affair, but at the same time he must have been somewhat relieved that Ian McBride had disappeared and not to be seen again."
"I'd call it convenient rather than relieved," Alistair remarked, partly under his breath.
"Wasn't any of this known until after his death?"
"I'm not sure but I don't think so. Bob Fairbrother certainly knew about it but I don't think he told the other officers until after Annie had spoken to him."
"Why did she do that I wonder?"
"To get at Charlie's wife, I suppose. It was probably Annie's way of getting her own back on Irene. She must have been very bitter. I do know that the two women never spoke to each other after that, and haven't done ever since."
"Both women still live in the same houses then?"
"Oh yes, and I've often seen them both in the Co-op at the same time and they completely ignore each other."
Alistair nodded knowingly. He had often encountered the same things in Glasgow during his investigations into cases. Women are funny creatures he concluded afterwards. Men would just punch each other on the nose or worse and then have a drink together in the local. He was thinking that when John came down from upstairs.
"I've got the notebook Alistair. Found the pages you want and you can read what I wrote at the time."
Alistair read John's notes but they revealed nothing more than he had already been told except for one observation. "You've put here…'Why don't we ask Charlie where he was at the time of Ian's disappearance?' Alistair looked at John. "Did anyone do that?"
"Not to my knowledge. You'll see it was my last note because it was soon after that, in fact it was the same afternoon, when the Chief called me in the office and I was moved off the case."

"Are you suggesting that if there was a cover-up the Chief was involved?"
"I did think so at the time but then dismissed it as extremely unlikely."
"It all seems very fishy to me."
"Ah! That's your professional experience now coming out Alistair, and your suspicious mind. But what you can't do now of course, is to question Charlie because he's buried somewhere in France!"
Alistair sat for a while looking thoughtful. "What I could do, is to have a word with both Annie McBride and Mrs Dimmick - I've forgotten already what you said her name was."
"Irene." Betty said and then thought that perhaps she should not encourage Alistair to do something that she felt wasn't right. "Do you think going to see them is wise, stirring things up after all this time? You may get on very well with Annie McBride, especially as you and your wife knew her and Ian so well, but I'm not sure about Irene Dimmick."
"Why not?"
"She's still a very attractive young woman. Joined the land army during the war and there were rumours, if you know what I mean?"
"Sounds just my type," Alistair quipped. He got up from his chair anxious to get on with what he wanted to do. "I agree that it may not be wise but it will satisfy me if I can discover that there was nothing to hide during the investigations. On the face of it, it does appear that it wasn't fully gone into at the time. I'll be very discreet and from what you have told me I understand there will be no danger of the two women comparing notes.
"I'll try to make my visits appear to be just courtesy calls." He then added for Betty's benefit, "But don't worry about me when I go to see Irene. I won't let her seduce me."
Betty looked shocked. "I didn't mean anything by that I just thought that you ought to know what she's like and not be taken by surprise."

Alistair gave her a kiss on the cheek and put a reassuring hand on her arm. "I'm sure I'll be alright," and grinned. He left hurriedly after thanking them both and telling John that he would not disclose the source of the information he had gained from his visit John shook his head after Alistair had gone.

"He won't find anything out you know, because there is nothing to find out, except the scandal and he knows about that now."

He looked at Betty. "Nothing about the affair was said at the inquest you know but the few of us who knew about it suspected that Ian McBride might have committed suicide ashamed of what he'd done."

CHAPTER THIRTY-NINE

Annie McBride was surprised when she opened the door and saw Alistair standing there. "Well I never! Alistair you old rascal. How lovely to see you. Come in."
"It may be a while since I was here last but you haven't changed a bit," Alistair lied unconvincingly. "I was in Paisley and thought there was no way I could go home without visiting one of my oldest friends. You may be a little older than when I last saw you but you're still as pretty as ever."
Annie put her hand to her hair, freshly permed that morning, which now had a few grey streaks starting to appear. "You old flatterer Alistair. Come and sit down. Isn't Judy with you?"
"No. I'm just here on my own. How's that young rogue of a son of yours?"
"David? Oh! He joined the Navy last year. Did his training in Plymouth and then joined HMS Illustrious. He's somewhere in the Mediterranean I think. His ship is hoping to come up here early next year to take part in the Review of the Fleet in the Clyde. I can't wait for him to come home."
"Not been made Commander of the Aircraft Carrier yet then?"
"You fool Alistair. Working in the stores, he told me in his last letter. Anyway how *is* Judy?"
"Judy? She's fine now she's got me at home to bully." He noticed that Annie's face had dropped a little and she was looking thoughtful. Alistair took advantage of the moment. "I expect David still misses his Dad."
"He doesn't ask about him now as he did for a long time afterwards. Ian's body was never found you know."
Alistair acknowledged that without saying a word. "I did follow some of the investigations at the time but being an ordinary copper I wasn't let in on everything."
Annie looked at him wondering whether he knew or not about her husband's goings on and if not, what he had meant by that remark.
"I didn't," he began and then hesitated, wondering how she would react if he mentioned what John had told him earlier. He then

decided that if he did not approach the subject now there might not be another opportunity so he finished the sentence. "I didn't hear about his indiscretion until much later."
Annie looked angry and clenched her fists. "That bloody woman was at the bottom of this. Ian would still be here if it hadn't been for her." She started to cry.
Alistair stood up and put his arm around her shoulders. "I'm sorry, Annie I shouldn't have said that. I'm sorry if I upset you. Here, dry your eyes." He gave her his handkerchief to use and was thankful that Judy had been thoughtful enough to give him a clean one before he left the house.
She wiped away the tears and straightened up as she returned his hankie. "Go back to your seat. I'm alright now. It was all kept very quiet at the time you know thanks to Bob Fairbrother, but I expect everyone knows about it now."
"Oh I don't believe anybody thinks badly of Ian for straying from the straight and narrow." He would like to have added, 'especially as she was such an attractive young woman,' but he thought better of it and left it at that.
"He did not stray as you put it. He was dragged away by her," Annie said forcibly and sounded angry again.
"I expect you're right. She was a flighty piece as I recall. I'm sorry again for getting things wrong."
"You obviously only know the half of it. Just sit there and relax while I go and make us a cup of tea - unless you'd like anything stronger," she added as an afterthought and then I'll tell you something.
"No. Tea will be fine. I've got used to not drinking while I'm on duty."
Annie stopped in her tracks, "On duty? I thought you'd retired Alistair."
Alistair laughed out loud to cover his embarrassing slip up. "I keep forgetting Annie, of course I've retired. What I meant, I suppose, is that not drinking during the day has become a habit."
"Well when I come back I'll tell you something that I expect you don't know."

Alistair was intrigued. It was all working out far better that he thought it would. What could she have possibly meant? He had a lot of questions he would have liked to have asked her but he would wait to see what she had to tell him first.
Annie brought two, full delicately decorated china teacups on a tray with some oatcakes she had made that morning. "I'm sorry I haven't any butter to put on them but I have managed to find a little margarine."
"I do remember that you used to make those oatcakes when we first knew you and I can say truthfully that I've never found anyone that can make them better than you. do"
"There you are again, you old flatterer. I suppose that is your way of getting people on your side so they can open their hearts to you."
It came quite naturally for Alistair to ask a question to get to the truth and he found himself doing so forgetting that Annie had already said that she would tell him something that perhaps he didn't know.
"Who was the last person to see Ian?" He didn't add the word 'alive' as he normally did because no one had seen him since.
"He went out after tea and just said he wouldn't be long. He told me he had some plants to pick up for the Poor House gardens. You knew he worked there didn't you?"
Alistair just nodded as he waited to hear what else she had to say.
"When it got late I began to worry and then as it became dark and he still hadn't come home I called round to the police station to see if anyone had seen him. I left little David in bed and asked my neighbour to come round and baby-sit. I saw Bob Fairbrother who said that he would visit a few pubs and try and find him but he was waiting for Charlie Dimmick to come back from a call he was on. I told him that I was worried and he promised to find him and make sure he went home."
"Didn't he see that you were worried?"
"I think he probably thought Ian was on a pub crawl. You know he did like a drink or two sometimes."

"Had you no idea where he had gone? Didn't you think he might have gone for a drink with the person he was going to meet?"
"Trouble was, Alistair, I suspected where he might have gone but I didn't want to believe it and was scared to go and find out."
"I think I can guess where you thought he might be."
"You see, I'd found out that he'd called round to Charlie Dimmick's house on a number of occasions to have a chat with Charlie he used to say, but I once found some lipstick on his collar after he had been there and another time I saw Charlie out with his Inspector when Ian was supposed to be visiting him."
"Didn't you tackle him about it? The lipstick I mean."
"He just said Irene had given him a kiss when he left and as he turned his head she kissed his collar."
"What about the time when you saw Charlie with his Inspector, which meant that Ian must have been at his house alone with his wife?"
"When he came home I did ask him if he'd had a nice chat with Charlie and he said 'Yes he had'."
"You knew that was a lie then."
"I didn't say anything, I just didn't want to believe what I was thinking. I hoped that if anything was going on it would just die out after a while."
"So when did you realise that it was becoming more serious?"
"I didn't realise it was going that way at first but as it got later and later that night and he still didn't turn up, I began to believe that he might have been with Irene Dimmick and worried that something might have happened to him after he left her."
Alistair had been completely in the dark about all this at the time and could hardly believe was Annie was telling him. "I didn't know about any of this the next morning when I went on duty. So what happened during the night?"
"Bob Fairbrother came round at about half past eleven and Charlie Dimmick came with him."
"Did Bob know what had been going on with your Ian and Charlie's wife?"

"I asked him outright if Ian had been at his house earlier in the evening and he assured me that he hadn't, but I always thought that both of them were hiding something from me."
"Why did you think that?" Alistair thought that perhaps this might give him a clue to the mystery.
"When I asked them if there was something they weren't telling me, Charlie said that his wife had seen Ian staggering down Moss Side by the dock as if he'd had too much to drink, but although Bob had asked all the pub landlords he couldn't find anyone who had served him with drink that night."
"I remember all that came out at the inquest and the coroner asked you if he ever took a bottle out with him and you said 'Never!"
"What was strange too Alistair, is that no one knew who the person was that Ian was supposed to be getting the plants from."
Alistair wanted to ask Annie something but was reluctant to do so at first but because it might have a bearing on what might have happened. Eventually he found the courage to ask. "Did you think that Ian was in love with Irene?"
"Infatuated perhaps, but in love, no!" she replied indignantly. "What ever made you ask that?"
"It was just a thought that if Ian was mixed up in his mind and didn't know what to do he might have done something...you know... silly"
"You mean, took his own life? Not Ian. He thought too much about David. He would never have done that."
Alistair began to regret he had asked the question. "The Coroner did ask if he might have committed suicide but it was dismissed out of hand and as you will remember, he brought in a verdict of 'missing, presumed drowned.'"
They both sat for a while without saying a word deep in thought, remembering the sad days that had followed. Alistair was the first to speak. "The police searched the river and docks for days and couldn't find him. I wonder what really happened? Have you ever thought about that?"

Annie gave a big sigh. "Continually at one time Alistair, but it's too late to worry about it now; Ian's gone and that's that."
Alistair was surprised by Annie's conclusions. It was not the sort of reaction he had expected to hear from her.
"I'm sorry, Annie, I hope you'll forgive me for talking for such a long time about that day and asking questions. I suppose I can't get used to holding a normal conversation with people."
"Well, you have been doing that sort of thing all you life haven't you."
Alistair got up to go. "I really must be getting back to my long-suffering wife. I did say that I wouldn't be long but I just wanted to pay a visit to my old friends and especially you."
Annie gave him a grin. "Well don't let this be the last time Alistair, and next time be sure Judy comes with you. Meanwhile give her my love."
Alistair left the house - not to go home as he had told Annie but to pay a visit to Charlie's widow.

CHAPTER FORTY

From the directions he had been given by John, Alistair soon found the house down Moss Road alongside the river and the door was opened almost before he had stopped knocking.
"Well, if it isn't Detective Inspector McIntosh. What brings you to Paisley?"
Irene Dimmick was still a very attractive woman. Alistair stood for a moment his eyes transfixed by her fresh unblemished face as she stood there smiling, looking at him with her wide-open bright blue eyes. Her blonde hair was neatly turned under and almost down to her shoulders. He found his voice at last.
"Now that I've retired I've come to Paisley looking up old friends and just wanted to see you for a moment to express my condolences on your loss of Charlie. I hadn't heard previously, but I saw George Craythorn at the police station and he told me"
Irene's expression changed from its first warm glow to a serious one. "I'm not the only one to lose a husband in the war but why don't you come in for a minute?"
"Well just for a minute. I was just on my way back to Glasgow and didn't want to go back without seeing you." Her invitation was playing right into his hands.
"Would you like a cup of tea or something?
Alistair thought that to accept would sound as if he had a reason for calling other than the one he had given. "Er, no, thank you. I've just had..." He suddenly realised that he had better not mention that he had been to see Annie McBride and stopped in mid-sentence. "I popped in to the cafe in the square just before I came here and had one there." He felt sure that she wouldn't check later whether his story had been true or not.
"What happened?
"To Charlie?"
Alistair nodded.
Irene sat down in the chair opposite to him and pulled her skirt down tightly over her unblemished bare knees appearing slightly nervous before answering his question.

"I don’t know really. It was soon after D Day that I had a telegram to say that Charlie had been killed by enemy action. Young David McBride in his PAMS uniform brought the telegram. I always felt sorry for that boy after losing his father."
The mention of David McBride gave Alistair the lead to ask her about Ian’s disappearance.
"Have you any idea what happened to his dad on that day he went missing?"
Irene looked up at Alistair and shook her head in a way that he had often seen people do when they had something to hide. He decided to be bold. "Did he not come to see you that evening Irene?" He asked the question in a quiet voice so that she would probably realise that he knew what had been going on.
"Oh! So you know."
Alistair wondered what she meant by that. Was she saying that she realised that he knew about the affair, or did she mean that he knew that Ian McBride had called to see her that evening he never arrived home. He decided to assume that she meant the latter.
"But didn't you tell the inquest that he hadn’t been to see you." Alistair paused wondering if he's gone too far."
Irene said nothing but stared down at the floor. He thought that he would risk another question. If he was mistaken she would fly up in the air and he would apologise.
"Why did you do that? And how long was he here?"
He asked the question in so quiet a voice that he wondered whether she had heard him.
"I suppose it doesn't matter now after all this time if I tell you the truth." She lifted up her head and looked straight at her inquisitor. "I couldn't tell the inquest any of that because of what Charlie did to Ian. You see, Charlie came home and caught us ...together."
Alistair could see that there was no need for him to ask any more questions. He knew she would now tell him what happened.
"Charlie laid into him and at one stage I thought he was going to hit me as well, but then he left to go back to the station with his parting words that if he saw Ian here again here he would kill him.

I tried to tidy him up as best I could. I wouldn't allow him go back to his wife in the state he was in."
"Was he badly hurt?"
"It was dark when he left and I saw him staggering down the road. I was frightened what would happen when he got home. I was very worried for him."
"Were you not scared what your husband would do to you when he came home?"
"I couldn't go to bed so I waited up, crying most of the time. Then finally, Charlie didn't come home until after midnight and he told me that he had discovered that Ian hadn't gone home and couldn't be found. The next day the search began with questions being asked and later police began dragging the river and so on as you know."
Alistair's mind was working hard following carefully what Irene was saying. He thought that there were a few pieces missing in her story. Either she had deliberately done so or had forgotten what had really happened.
"Did you say that Charlie didn't come back until after midnight to see if Ian was still here?"
"I doubt if he thought Ian would still be here, but I thought that strange afterwards why he was so late coming back. We talked for a long time during the night neither of us getting much sleep. He then said that it would be best if we didn't say anything about Ian being here as it would get him into serious trouble if it came out that he had beaten him up and that he would certainly lose his job and I too would have been in disgrace."
"Did Bob Fairbrother know about what Charlie did to Ian McBride?"
Irene was quick to answer. "No, I'm sure he didn't. Charlie would have told me if he had."
Alistair's suspicious mind was in overdrive. But if Bob had known then it might explain why nothing was said. After all, the truth would never be discovered if Ian's body was never found. Could they have murdered Ian together? No surely not...and yet?

"I wonder what really happened to Ian McBride," Alistair said more to himself than out loud.
"When I eventually went though Charlie's papers I did find a letter addressed to me in an envelope marked 'Not to be opened until after my death.' There was a separate piece of paper which referred to that day."
"Can I ask what was on that paper?"
"I'll fetch it. It's upstairs."
She gave Alistair the paper without saying a word. It read:-
"Dear Irene, Do not tell anyone what happened on that day when Ian disappeared. It will only cause you misery if other people discovered that he'd been with you all that evening. As you know, I lost my temper at the time and felt I wanted to kill him and I did it because I could not bear to think of anyone taking you away from me. We were lucky that his body was never found and don't think that it ever will be, so don't worry about it. Love Charlie."
Alistair read it two or three times trying to make out what Charlie had meant by the passage -
"I did it because I could not bear to think of anyone taking you away from me." He wondered what he was really saying when he wrote, "I did it". Did what? Beat him up? - or kill him? He said in the letter that he wanted to kill him and why did he write, "we were lucky that the body was never found?" Did he know that it wouldn't be? There were a lot of unanswered questions in that letter, but with Charlie gone, there was no one to ask, except perhaps Bob Fairbrother! He realised, however, that Bob would not say anything because if he had known what Charlie had done then he would not reveal it now, for his own sake. But what of Irene?
"Do you really not know what happened to Ian?" he asked her finally, and was hoping that she would tell more to enable him to get at the truth. He found himself asking the question in exactly the same way that he would have done if he had still been in his old job as a Detective Inspector.
Irene appeared disturbed, suddenly realising that she had told Alistair too much already. "No. I don't know," she said in the

same abrupt manner that Alistair had asked the question. "Perhaps I shouldn't have given you that letter to read. He did tell me not to tell anyone and now you've been the first one, apart from me, to see it and if you tell anyone I'll just deny that it ever existed. Charlie's gone now as well as Ian and that's that, so let's now forget it after all this time".
She then stood up and made a business of looking at the clock on the mantelpiece. "I'm afraid that you must excuse me Alistair. I have arranged to meet one or two of the girls I work with at the scarf factory and I must get ready to go out."
Alistair took this to be a hint for him to leave. He thanked her for being honest with him and assured her that he would not tell anyone of their conversation and would do as she had suggested and forget it, but as he walked back to his car he knew that he had no intention of keeping the promise that he had just made.

Driving away from the house, he thought that it was amazing that none of this had come out at the time. Surely Inspector Bob Fairbrother who had investigated the case should have put two and two together unless, of course, he was involved in the conspiracy. Then he remembered that there had been very little said or even discussed about Ian's disappearance at the time and the conclusion was reached very quickly that he must have fallen into the river and been carried out to sea. The evidence given about Irene seeing him staggering home because he was drunk he could now refute. It was obviously due to the fact he had taken a hammering from her husband, Charlie, which caused him to find walking difficult. That was the reason why no publican could be found who had served him drinks as first thought at the inquest.
He pulled his car to the side of the road and switched off the engine.
He wondered how many others had known about the beating that Ian had endured? Alistair decided that someone must have deliberately kept that from the Chief Superintendent unless he also knew about it and decided to keep quiet. A decision was probably reached to hush it up so as not to ruin Charlie's career. After all,

some may have thought that he was justified in beating up his wife's lover. Inspector Bob Fairbrother had certainly lied, or been told to keep quiet about seeing Ian that evening but the Chief must have surely known. Alistair also thought that Sergeant John McCloud must have suspected that someone was not telling the truth. It certainly would explain why he was moved off the case as soon as he started to ask awkward questions.

He started the engine of his car and then switched it off again as he suddenly thought of something else.

He began to consider another possible but bizarre alternative. Could Charlie have picked Ian up in the police car with the purpose of taking him home? It would be doubtful if anybody would see him as it was very late and the streets were quiet at that time of night? Had Ian then perhaps have a heart attack in the car and died? If he then took him home to Annie what would she have thought when she saw that her dead husband had been badly beaten up? Surely Charlie would panic if that had been the case and have decided on the spur of the moment to drive to a remote spot to get rid of the body? He was very late getting home according to Irene! It would be a simple solution, but Alistair then dismissed this idea thinking it too ridiculous to contemplate. But, of the other hand, he said to himself as he drove away, it seemed a better explanation than the one given at the inquest that the body was no doubt carried out to the Clyde after allegedly falling in the river Cart, an event which had always seemed to be unlikely to happen.

He was certain now that the last person he would have to talk to was Bob Fairbrother but he wanted more time to think about that. If Bob knew more than he had let on at the time then it would be doubtful if he would admit to it now. So would there be any point in seeing him? Alistair decided he would go home and try to digest what he had already learned from all the people he had interviewed.

CHAPTER FORTY-ONE

Judy was ironing when he got home. "Well. Have you had a good day and solved the mystery?" She was certain that her husband would not have found out anything new and that nothing would have come from his investigations.
The retired Detective Inspector knew that his wife was being flippant and delighted in telling her that she would be surprised at what he had found out. "I discovered that Ian was beaten up on that evening when he disappeared and you'll never guess by whom."
"By Charlie Dimmick, I shouldn't wonder," Judy suggested without looking up from her ironing.
Alistair stared at his wife his mouth wide open, unable to speak. He tried to choose the right words when he recovered from the shock, "But why should you. ...?"
Judy didn't let him finish his question. "Were you going to ask me why I thought it was him? Because, my dear husband, Annie had told me in confidence that Ian was seeing Irene but asked me not to tell anyone, especially you. I'd thought nothing more about it until now."
"But it should have been your duty to tell. You were holding back information vital to the investigations and it should have come out at the inquest!"
Judy banged down the iron on the table. "Now see here, Alistair. There was nothing at the time to suggest Ian had been there that night, in fact, Irene denied it as I recall, so why should I have broken my word to Annie? You've only just found out that Ian and Charlie fought, if that's what happened, and when you asked me who it was that beat him up, as you put it, I naturally assumed that it would have been Charlie. It's plain to me that Charlie was the one that held back vital information not me and him a policeman at that!"
Alistair realised that his criticism of his wife had been unfair. "Yes. You're right Judy. I'm sorry. I can see the reason why no one said anything about it, but knowing what I know now there

was certainly a cover-up not only by Charlie and Irene, but Bob Fairbrother and others and almost certainly the Chief as well!"
"So you know now what happened to Ian then?"
"Well no not really. I've got to do a bit more investigating."
Judy glared at him astonished. "Oh! no you don't Alistair McIntosh." She picked up the piece of paper that her husband had written on before he left to go to Paisley and laid it out before him. "Read this! You made a promise that you'd take me on holiday after you'd been to Paisley and I'm going to make you keep to it. I don't want to hear about any more of your useless investigations."

CHAPTER FORTY-TWO

Judy and Alistair arrived in Oban of the west coast of Scotland early September and everywhere was quiet. The sun was low on the horizon although it had been quite a warm day for the time of the year. They knew that in Scotland, September and May, often were the best two months for fine weather and it appeared that it was going to live up to its reputation. Judy was thrilled to be in the coastal town that she had not visited since long before the war. They found a small guesthouse not far from the harbour and were greeted by a red-faced lady of about Judy's age but of a more rounded appearance.
"Will ye be stayin' long?" she asked with a broad welcoming smile.
Judy got in before Alistair could speak in case he was about to tell her 'only a day or two.' "We'll be here for a week. If that's alright with you."
"Then I'll need your ration books if you don't mind."
"Of course." Judy took them out of her handbag and gave them to her.
"I'll only take as little as I need to. I do hope you like fish as we have a good selection here as you can imagine and thank goodness we don't need points for those." She gave quite a loud chuckle and opened the guest book looking at Alistair as she did so. "If you'd put your names and address in here please and then I'll show you to your room. I've got a nice bedroom at the front, which'll giv'ye a good view right over the sea to the Isle of Mull."
Alistair went to the car to get the two heavy cases from the back seat and hoped that he would be able to struggle up the stairs with them without pulling a muscle. On second thoughts he wondered if he did so Judy might then cancel the holiday and hopefully they would return home. However, he decided that he would be careful as he did not particularly look forward to suffering the inevitable pain that it would cause.

The first three days they had fine sunny weather and made the most of the warm sunshine. They took the ferry to Mull on Monday morning and spent some time exploring Duart Castle and wandering round that part of the island. Judy was fascinated to learn all about the old 13th century stronghold which was now the home of the Chief of the Clan McLean, while Alistair's patience wore thin as time went by and he was thankful when it was time to catch the ferry back to Oban.

He was much more interested in watching the boats coming in laden with the fish the next morning and the fishermen in their oilskin coats unloading their catches. Judy preferred to sit on a bench and watch the antics of the sea birds while Alistair spent some time talking to the fishermen. The crabs and lobsters took his attention and when one of the men scooped up the black eggs from under the belly of a female lobster and gave it to him to eat, he thought that the taste was as near to caviar as he could imagine it to be. He found it much more enjoyable talking to the men and hearing about their experiences at sea than looking around castles and he was going to make the most of it while he had chance.

Judy had already told him that she wanted to go to the little granite cathedral next day and explore the ruins of Dunollie Castle, which was nearby. She'd also said that she'd like to visit to his horror, yet another castle, Dunstaffnage, as well as McCaig's Folly overlooking the town. Mrs McTavish, their landlady had told them that it was a fine view across the Firth of Lorn from the top of Pulpit Hill so that was another of Judy's priorities.

Alistair was beginning to tire of looking at old monuments and ruins but he thought that perhaps a view across the Firth would be a change from more castle exploring. What he really wanted was to ride along Loch Awe and, while Judy was visiting more buildings he could watch the men fishing for trout.

That evening after Mrs McTavish had given them an excellent lobster meal they set off to spend an hour or so in the local pub not far from the house. They thought that it would be interesting to mix with the locals and get some of the atmosphere with the local people of Oban.

Going to the bar to order their drinks, Alistair accidentally caught the elbow of a young man sitting on a stool. His apology was accepted and they began a friendly and informal conversation. The man introduced himself as Bill McKern. Alistair had thought that when he came here he would be able get away from being reminded of his last case that involved a soldier called McKern. "I was just smiling when you told me your name because I recently knew a soldier called McKern in Glasgow."

"Och, that's quite an ordinary name in these parts."

"He wasn't very ordinary; he got murdered."

The man stared at Alistair as if in shock. "Do you mean Andy McKern? He was my brother. How did you know him?"

Alistair sat down on the stool next him and looked closely at the man's face. He thought he had seen him before and realised that he must have been at Andy's funeral. He told him that he was the detective who had investigated the murders.

"We never had much in common and I was told about his death from the Army Authorities. They had me down as his next of kin. There was nothing I could have said at the inquest, so I didn't bother to attend but I did go to his funeral and paid for it"

Alistair felt a bit uncomfortable. "I'm sorry I didn't find out about you. I retired from the police soon afterwards"

"But you will know then what really happened. I only read the reports in the National newspapers, which left a lot of questions unanswered. For instance, why did someone who was supposed to be his friend kill my brother? The report said that a chap called Cope had visited Andy when he was in hospital recovering from an operation on his arm after being wounded in Germany. What was hard to bear was the way my brother had died, especially after what he'd been through during the war. If it was robbery, which appeared to be the motive, where did my brother get all that money? And who was that American soldier that it was reported that Cope had killed?"

Alistair knew of course, that the police had told the reporters only the bare facts about the murders mainly to protect the girl and her

Royal Navy boyfriend who they thought had been involved quite innocently.
"Well I must admit Bill, I only had to investigate the murders. It appeared that it was the American soldier's money in the first place and we concluded that he was murdered by Cope who we believed was at one time a friend of your brother."
"Some friend!" Bill exclaimed
Alistair continued. "It appears that the money was split between the two of them and Cope murdered your brother in order to get the lot. We have not been able to find out where the money came from although it was in Scottish notes. As your brother had some of the money in his possession before he was killed, then I'm afraid that he might have been involved with the American's murder, although we believe that it was Cope who did him in as both murders were done in the same way. There's no one left to ask, I'm afraid."
Bill looked thoughtful. "I thought Andy's old business friend might have been involved, but then dismissed it as he wasn't at the funeral, which still seemed strange to me."
"His old friend, did you say? Who was that?"
"Old Charlie MacKenzie. Andy worked at another jeweller's before the war but the shop was bombed and his old employer died in the raid, but he was always in and out of Mr Mackenzie's shop. You probably know who I mean. The jeweller in Sauchiehall Street if he's still there. I think he used to be in Charlie's shop more often than where he was supposed to be working in his own."
Alistair sat bolt upright on the stool. "Would this Charlie MacKenzie have been interested in diamonds?"
"Oh! sure. Charlie was an expert on diamonds. Andy used to tell me that he learnt a lot about diamonds before going into the army and that Charlie MacKenzie taught him all he knew about the subject."
Alistair was aware that behind him a female voice was speaking to him in rather a firm manner.
"Am I going to have a drink or not?"

"It's diamonds Judy. The missing link is Charlie MacKenzie in Sauchiehall Street."
"Is this Charlie, what ever you call him, going to buy me a drink then?" Judy said sarcastically.
"No! I'm sorry, my love. I've been talking to this gentleman. He's Andy's brother. What did you say you wanted to drink?"

CHAPTER FORTY-THREE

Alistair couldn't wait to get home and to contact Sergeant Baillie. He left a message with the duty officer at Glasgow Central station in Renfield Street for him to come and see him as soon as possible as he has some important information to give him. Alistair was feeling quite smug in view of the new discovery he had made in regard to his last case. It would still need to be investigated even if turned out to be not relevant to the money or the murder of the American soldier, but he wondered if there could be a connection between the jeweller he had been told about and the diamond that the sailor had in his possession. He had always thought that the explanation given by Howard Hartwell was too good to be true.
Alistair knew of course, that as he was now not part of the force he would not be able to do anything about it himself, but he was going to enjoy watching others acting on the information he would give them.
It was late in the afternoon when Sergeant Baillie called.
Alistair greeted him at the door. "Come in Robert." Judy was in the kitchen. He called out to her. "Judy! It's Robert. Put the kettle on. I'm sure he would like a cup of tea."
"How was your holiday?" the sergeant asked. "Did you enjoy Oban? How was the weather?"
"I've trained you well," Alistair said laughing. "Full of questions. Yes, we had quite a good time, but I believe Judy enjoyed it more than I did but it was a nice break. We both pleased that we chose Oban and I, even more pleased than Judy. The weather was mixed as usual at this time of year on the West coast."
Robert ignored the implication of the remark he made about being more pleased than his wife as he knew that his old inspector would tell him in his own good time. It would no doubt be connected to the important information he had been told he had.
"Well, at least you got away from thinking about crime and unsolved cases."
Alistair looked at his old sergeant with a faint smile on his lips and said nothing for a minute.

Robert Baillie could tell that his old boss was enjoying delaying this information he was about to reveal and did not need two guesses that it would be connected to his last case. He knew his old Inspector too well.
Judy brought in cups of tea on a tray with some ginger nut biscuits. "How are you, Robert? He's been dying to see you from the middle of last week. I had an awful job preventing him from coming home earlier."
"Tea alright, Robert? Sweet enough?" Alistair was teasing his old colleague.
"Oh, for goodness sake Alistair, what is it you want to tell me?" he thought that if he addressed him in a less official manner he would get on with what he wanted to say.
"I'm sorry, Robert. It's just that I've learnt something while I've been away and I know that you're going to be excited to hear what I've discovered."
Robert frowned in bewilderment.
"You remember the soldier who was murdered by Corporal Sidney Cope?"
"Andy McKern! Would I ever forget seeing him lying there dead as a Dodo when we went to question him."
"I spoke to his brother who lives in Oban and you'll never guess where McKern worked before he went in the army."
Robert looked closely at his old inspector trying to read his thoughts. "Don't tell me that it was at a jewellers."
Alistair was taken aback. What had been meant to be a surprise, Robert had anticipated.
"You're right! Whatever made you guess that?"
"I thought for a second that you meant he worked in a bank but then I remembered the diamond and put two and two together. You forget sir, that I've worked with you for a long time and you left me with one thing to solve - well, two really. Where the diamond that the sailor sold came from and the source of all that money. I've always thought that Howard and Elizabeth's version of where the diamond came from was suspect, so now we might discover the truth."

"I don't suppose you can now guess which jeweller's clever clogs" Alistair asked him in a rather sarcastic manner.
Robert spread out his arms hands turned upwards and shrugged his shoulders. "No. But you're about to tell me."
"It was the jeweller's shop in the area close to the docks, which was destroyed in a bombing raid."
His old sergeant frowned wondering how that could be of use and if his old boss had lost his marbles.
"Now, before you say that won't help us much," Alistair continued, "Andy's brother told me that he was very friendly with another jeweller."
Robert began to look more interested." Who was that then?"
"One of the jewellers you called at no doubt, when you were making enquiries. Charlie MacKenzie in Sauchiehall Street."
Robert did remember calling there and remembered that the old jeweller had appeared quite nervous when he had questioned him, but had put it down to his age. "So you think that the diamond may have come from his shop."
"It don't know. It could be. It would be a more believable explanation but it will give you a lead. I thought you'd be pleased."
Robert sat in deep thought as he sipped his tea. "Do you think that Charlie MacKenzie was also involved with the large amount of cash we discovered as well?"
"I don't know that either Robert. It's your duty to go and find that out when you question him. I wish I was still on the force and I would enjoy going to see him."
Judy nearly jumped out of the seat she was sitting in. "Well I'm pleased you're not still on the force." She had been listening quietly to what was going on and ready to pounce if Alistair went too far. "You've told Robert what you discovered in Oban and you have now passed on the information as you said you would. Now leave it to Robert."
Alistair realised that he'd have to leave it at that. "Still, I would interested to know how you get on. Perhaps your new boss, Brian Hunter will be pleased. I expect he'll go to the shop with you."

Baillie got up ready to leave now anxious to get back to his new Chief Inspector. "He is familiar with the case and I'm sure he will be pleased with this new information and to try and tie up those loose ends we left undone."
After a few more pleasantries, Alistair wished his old sergeant the best of luck and watched him move away in the old police car.

"Now I can get on with looking at what happened to poor old Ian McBride," he said sitting back in his chair.
Judy sighed. "Oh, I wish you would leave that alone. I can't possibly see what you are trying to achieve after all this time. Without a body you'll never be able to prove anything."
Alistair picked up his newspaper. He did not wish to discuss it any further. He knew that however long they went over the reasons as to why he was still interested, Judy would never understand what he was trying to do or why.

CHAPTER FORTY-FOUR

Three days later Alistair was back in Paisley. He had telephoned George Craythorn, the sergeant at the police station and arranged to meet him at Gilmore Street Railway Station. He parked his car in the station yard and found George sitting on a bench outside the waiting room.

George looked surprised when he saw Alistair approaching "I thought that you might be coming in on the train, Was that the reason why you wanted me to meet you here? but why all the secrecy, Alistair?"

"I just didn't want anyone else to know that I was coming or why. I thought that if I called at the police station others would become suspicious especially that Inspector of yours."

"How are you getting on with your investigations? Any developments so far? Did you see all the people you wanted to when you were last here?"

"I'll keep the answers to your first two questions to myself for the time being George, but as to the last one, I saw them all but one. And that's why I've come back. I certainly learned more than I knew previously but there's still a mystery as to what happened after Ian left Charlie Dimmick's house."

"What do you mean, 'left Charlie's house'? What was he doing there? I thought it was said that he was going to get some plants from a friend!"

Alistair had let slip where Ian had been without realising that George knew nothing about Ian's secret meetings with Irene Dimmick. He knew now he would have to tell him all that he had discovered.

George sat quietly as Alistair told him the whole story.

"That's incredible," he exclaimed when Alistair had finished. "I can't believe that nothing was known or said by anyone at the time. Do you believe that Charlie Dimmick murdered Ian McBride then?"

"That's what I'm hoping to find out, but I don't have much hope of doing so. Charlie's dead and there's no way of finding Ian's body after all this time so I'm left with only a last resort."
"Which is I presume", George observed, "to find out if Bob Fairbrother knew what Charlie did to Ian and also what else he knew."
"Correct!" That's my only hope to conclude the matter."
"But if Bob admits to both those things, which I can't see him doing, but if he did know, won't that lead to an investigation and possible criminal proceedings against the people concerned? Including Irene who lied at the inquest; Bob himself by withholding information and probably maybe others who knew and possibly the Chief?"
George looked very hard at his old friend. "Bloody hell Alistair, a lot of people could get hurt!"
Alistair smiled and put a reassuring hand on the sergeant's shoulder. "Whatever I discover in addition to what I already now know, I won't be able to prove a thing. I've already learned the truth about a lot of things, which now make sense and even if Bob does admit that he knew that Charlie killed Ian, which, as you say, I doubt that he'll do, there would be no way that I would go into the witness box and swear to what I know or have been told. Everyone will deny it anyway and I would look a perfect fool."
"I can see that thank goodness," George admitted.
"In addition," Alistair went on, " But if it could be proved that Charlie was Ian's murderer and all of this came out, it wouldn't do the police any good to be the centre of a scandal, Ian's wife would be embarrassed to say the least, Irene would be disgraced and Bob and others would probably lose their pensions! The only person that would not get hurt would be Charlie himself, who would be looking down at the proceedings from above and have a gratifying smile on his face knowing that we could do nothing to him.
"Perhaps it was justice that he was killed in France," George remarked..
"Now just a minute George my boy, you're jumping the gun. Charlie Dimmick is probably innocent and is only guilty of giving

Ian a good hiding for having it off with his wife, if that is what he had been doing and Charlie did only what probably you or I would have done if we had been in his position."
"Except that he lied."
"Admitted that he didn't tell the truth, but would we have done the same in the circumstances? If he hadn't murdered Ian, would anyone have believed that he wasn't involved in his murder if he'd admitted to beating him up on the same evening that he'd disappeared?"
George looked at his watch and stood up quickly. "Look I've got to get back on duty so I'll leave you to carry on with your investigations. Let me know how you get on. You've made me very curious" He turned to go.
"Just two things before you leave me George. I hadn't intended to tell you about any of this, so firstly, I want you to promise me that you will keep all this to yourself and not breathe a word to anyone. Secondly, the main reason I wanted you to meet me was for you to give me Bob Fairbrother's address."

CHAPTER FORTY-FIVE

Alistair spent the rest of the morning contemplating how best to approach Bob Fairbrother. If he began by asking questions about what he thought Charlie was doing on the night in question it would only be an invitation for Bob to keep what he knew to himself. If he were to deny any knowledge of what went on, Alistair knew that would be the end of his enquiry and he would find out nothing. On the other hand, if he let slip that he knew more than Bob would have expected him to know, then he might be able to get him to talk more freely about what happened.
He knew that Bob would be surprised to see him especially as it had been such a long time since they met and had nothing in common. The last thing Bob Fairbrother would expect was to be questioned about Ian McBride's disappearance, least of all by someone who was only a P.C. at the time and not even involved in the case. Retiring as a senior rank officer to Bob Fairbrother, Alistair knew that he would not be brushed aside when he started to ask him some questions but he would try to make it look as though he was just being inquisitive.
He knew one thing that he would ask him for certain. Wasn't he suspicious about the length of time that Charlie was away from the Station? Also he would ask him whether he had he known all along that Charlie had discovered Ian with his wife. If he had known this, then it would be more than likely that he had also been aware that Charlie had attacked Ian. He could go on speculating all day without getting anywhere so he would have to go and see him with a clear mind and be optimistic about the results.
He had been sitting in the cafe eating his fish and chip lunch while he was doing all this thinking. Looking down at the empty plate where he had placed his knife and fork neatly side by side, he had been so absorbed with his thoughts he had a job trying to recall what he had actually eaten. The little ginger-haired waitress came to remove his plate and brought him the cup of coffee that he had previously ordered. He left a florin on the table, which included a

tip for the young girl, and now, sustained by the generous-sized meal he had eaten, set off with the hope that Bob Fairbrother would be at home.
Bob answered the door and looked genuinely surprised to see him standing there. Alistair hardly recognised him. He had shaved off his moustache and lost most of his hair. He had put on a considerable amount of weight since he last saw him but his bald head seemed in keeping with his portly figure.
"Good god! Alistair McIntosh. What are you doing in this neck of the woods?"
"Coming to see you, obviously."
"Well come in. You've just missed Pearl. She's gone shopping and didn't say how long she'd be."
The two men chatted for a while about the old times and got up to date with their lives. Then Alistair thought it was time to approach the subject he had come about without making it too obvious why he was there.
"You know Bob," he began, "I still think about poor old Ian and often wonder what happened to the poor old chap. He was such a nice fellow."
Bob nodded, which Alistair took to be an agreement with his sentiments. Bob was looking down at the floor but said nothing.
"I know he had his faults and weaknesses as we all have," Alistair continued as he tried to get some reaction from his ex-colleague, "but to disappear as he did was a mystery." Still Bob did not move from the position he was in.
Alistair decided to surprise him to try and get him to respond. "We know of course, that he was visiting Charlie's wife on occasions and I expect that Charlie was none too pleased about that."
He got the reaction he expected. Bob was staring at Alistair. "I didn't know you knew about that. I thought that no one knew except Pearl and..."
"You, the Chief, and me." Alistair took a risk in saying that but he received no denial.
"But when did you know?"

"You forget that we were very friendly with the McBrides. Annie confided in my Judy from the day it all started." That was true, of course, but he didn't reveal that he had only found out from his wife recently. Bob looked a little confused and frowned as he tried to take in the revelation. Alistair took advantage of this.
"I think if I'd have been Charlie, I would have given Ian a good hiding for messing with my wife. Is that what you think he did Bob? It would explain why someone thought that he was drunk when Irene said that she saw him staggering down the road later that night?"
"I, I, don't know", Bob spluttered, still at a loss to as to how much Alistair knew. " Perhaps he did."
"It doesn't matter now Bob, does it? Charlie's dead so whatever he did doesn't matter.
He now thought that he's ask George a direct question to see how he would react. "How long was he away from the station that night? I know you had to wait for him to return after Annie had reported Ian missing. Where did you think he'd been?"
Bob was beginning to feel that Alistair knew more than he was admitting to and did not quite know how to answer his question. If he lied perhaps Alistair would know that he was lying.
"He didn't say exactly, except that he said it was in regard to a complaint he had received. He took the police car as he said the call came from a house some way away past the Park on the Glasgow Road."
"Did he tell you where it was when he got back? Did he enter anything in the desk book?"
"I don't know I never checked," Bob answered cautiously.
"But you did know Charlie had been to his home and found Ian there?"
Bob looked shocked and felt the blood rushing to his cheeks. How much does this man know? he thought. "He had some blood on his jacket and shirt when he came back and admitted to me what he'd done. I don't understand how you know all this. Have you been to see Irene?"

Alistair ignored the question and wanted to continue now that Bob was off guard.
"You mean that he did beat him up"
"Probably, and then added quickly, "I don't really know."
Alistair was not convinced that Bob didn't know. "When you both went out again looking for Ian, did you go together?"
"No. I went to the pubs and Charlie went off in the car again. What are you suggesting?"
"I'm suggesting nothing, Bob. I just think that they may have been another reason why Ian's body was never found."
"What do you mean? Charlie ran him down and took the body to the Clyde and dumped him in there?" He paused, staring straight at Alistair waiting for any reaction.
"No. That sounds too ridiculous for words," Alistair continued, " but we will never know will we? Then again if he did something like that it would be a very good reason why Ian's body has never been found."
Bob suddenly wished he had never said that and was now anxious to make sure that Alistair believed that he had nothing to do with Ian's disappearance. He began to worry if Alistair was beginning to believe that he wasn't telling the truth.
"Look Alistair, I knew about Charlie finding Ian with Irene and I did know that he gave him a good hiding but that's all I know. I have no idea what happened to Ian. Falling in the river sounded at the time to be the only possible explanation and still does."
"I take it then that the confrontation was all hushed up to save embarrassment for both Annie and Irene and the adverse publicity that would have ensued if it was known that one policeman had beaten up another."
Bob was beginning to feel a little more comfortable and regained his composure. "Exactly. There was a brief enquiry at the station but when no body could be found it was assumed that Ian had fallen into the river Cart and been taken out to sea with the tide. There was little point in making the scandal public. That's why everyone who knew kept quiet and, as you know, the Coroner brought the inquest to a conclusion quite quickly by deciding that

Ian's body was missing, presumed drowned. You've just told me that you and your wife knew about Ian and Irene but now what I don't understand, is why you didn't cause trouble at the inquest instead of keeping silent. "
Alistair had to think quickly, bearing in mind that it was only a recent revelation. "I knew nothing about the enquiry if you remember. I was only an ordinary copper at the time and didn't even attend the inquest. But I just told you. We were close friends with Annie McBride and kept our word that we wouldn't say anything about Ian's indiscretions. Alright?" Alistair was finding it surprisingly easy to lie, but he was worried that Bob might ask some more awkward questions and thought it time to take his leave. He got up from his chair and stuck out his hand. "It's been great seeing you again Bob, and chatting about old times. Give my love to Pearl and tell her that I'm sorry I missed her."
He left in a hurry as Bob was contemplating what Alistair had made him admit to. As he closed the door he began to wonder if Alistair and his wife, Judy, had really known about Ian's affair with Irene? Or was it guesswork on his part to make him admit what he knew? He suddenly realised that he had told Alistair about the confrontation between Charlie and Ian and not the other way round! Alistair had not answered his question when had had asked him if Charlie's wife Irene, had told him about it. He began to doubt everything that Alistair had said and was realising that he had given him much more information about what had happened on that night than Alistair had given him.
"The crafty old bugger," he remarked to himself as he sat down heavily in his favourite chair.
On the way home Alistair reflected on what he considered to be a fairly fruitful enquiry. Bob had given him the answers to a number of things that had been puzzling him about including whether he knew about Ian's movements on the night when he had disappeared. If Charlie had done what Bob had light-heartedly suggested - ran him down in a fit of temper and then, realizing that he had killed him - took him to a place further up the river

and thrown him in, it would explain why the body had never been found.
If Charlie had dumped Ian's body for whatever reason there was no way he could prove it because Charlie was dead! And there would be no chance of finding a body after all this time. If he had killed Ian and dumped the body did Bob know what Charlie had done?
Alistair's mind was working overtime, just as he done all his life trying to solve murders, but suddenly realised what he was doing. These were not common criminals he was investigating, they were fellow policemen! No bobbies in their right minds would do what he was contemplating they might have done. Charlie Dimmick would never have got away with dumping Ian McBride's body, or that any of his fellow officers would have covered for him, least of all the Chief! But because of his experience in questioning people in similar circumstances there was no question in his mind that Bob Fairbrother had been hiding something from him.
Alistair drove on, anxious to get home and resigned to the fact that nothing else could be done. It would remain an unsolved mystery but at least he had tried.

CHAPTER FORTY-SIX

During the last part of the journey, he wondered how his old sergeant was getting on with questioning Charlie MacKenzie the jeweller in Sauchiehall Street with regard to the murders of the American G.I. and the soldier. He smiled as he imagined how Robert and his new detective inspector would get on without him. I bet they make a balls-up of it, he said to himself conceitedly.
Judy was pleased to see him come back home from his adventures in Paisley. "Well now, have you done all that you wanted to do? Is this the end to all your gallivanting off to Paisley?"
Alistair didn't answer but put his hands on her shoulders and gave her a big kiss.
She was taken by surprise. "Now what was that for? Are you so pleased with yourself that it's your way of thanking me for letting you go and get rid of your obsession with poor Ian McBride?"
Alistair took off his coat and hung it up on the peg in the hall then turned to face his wife and shrugged his shoulders. Judy felt a cold shudder go through her body. So he was still to go on with it, she thought.
"If you'd make me a cup of tea, I'll tell you the whole story."
So far he had kept most of what he'd found out during his investigations from her, but now he thought it was only right that she should know what his conclusions were in the case. He still described every problem that needed solving as a 'case'. He sat down slowly in his favourite armchair, placed his elbows on his knees and formed a pyramid with his fingers as he recalled all that had happened. Judy brought the tea into the room on a tray. Pouring out two cups, she handed one to Alistair then sat down herself on the edge of her chair and rested her hands into her lap. "Right, I'm ready. Tell me all."
Alistair then told her everything he had discovered about what had happened that night when Ian had disappeared. "So you see" he concluded, "there's nothing else I can find out. It was either an accident or he was murdered by Charlie. We'll never know and I don't believe that anyone else knew either so that's the end of it."

"Thank goodness for that," Judy remarked when he had said the final word. "And now we can get on with enjoying your retirement. No more police work."
Alistair put down his cup after drinking his tea. "Well, there's just one more thing."
Judy closed her eyes and shook her head in despair. "Oh! no. Now what?"
"It's not very much and I won't be involved. I just want to know how Robert went on with his enquiries from the information I gave him after speaking to McKern's brother in Oban."
Judy realised that as usual it was no use trying to talk him out of something he had set his heart on. "Well, if that's all you are going to do, then I won't mind. But after that, promise me, no more."
"I promise," he said humbly.
Alistair was restless. When Judy wasn't around he kept leaping from his chair and looking at of the window. Robert must have found something out by now he said to himself so why had he not called to let him know the outcome? As the day wore on he went into his garden and pottered around doing odd jobs that required attention. He cut down some of the dead flower stalks in his herbaceous border, dead-headed the roses then dug up a root of potatoes putting the tops on the compost heap. He expected that at any moment Judy would call to him telling him that Robert had arrived. During the evening he put away the thought of anyone coming as he enjoyed an episode of ITMA on the wireless. Aware of his disappointment, Judy made him a nice cup of Ovaltine to take to bed and he poured himself a generous measure of scotch to go with it.
"I think that the whisky should send me off more than the hot drink," he told Judy taking the cup in the one hand and carrying the glass in the other, but he woke up in the early hours and could hardly wait until it got light when he would be able to get up and make a cup of tea for them both. Surely Robert would come today, but if he didn't, he promised himself that he would ring the station and ask if he was there. If not, he would leave a message to

say he had rung. That would prompt Robert to come and tell him the result of his interview with Charlie MacKenzie.
He had just finished reading the "Glasgow Herald" when Robert arrived. He let Judy answer the door and when Robert walked in Alistair rose from his chair slowly so as not to let him think that he was expecting him, "Oh! This is a surprise. I thought that you'd be too busy to come and visit your old Inspector so soon. To what do we owe the pleasure of this call?"
Judy was speechless. She was bursting to say something but was so taken aback by her husband's pretence that she had to go quickly into the kitchen before she exploded with laughter.
"Well, Alistair," Robert began as he sat down, "That old jeweller knew nothing, so he said. He told me that when I first visited him that he knew Andy McKern but had not seen him since he went into the army. He had read about him being murdered but didn't attend his funeral because there was no one to look after the shop."
"What about the American? Had he been to his shop?"
"No. He reminded me that it was I who told him about the American being murdered when I first interviewed him at one of the jewellers you asked me to visit when we making enquiries. He knew nothing about diamonds being sold or bought then or since. He also said that the only time an American soldier had been in his shop was this July."
"That was about the time when they came back to persuade their sweethearts to go back with them to the US as their wives," Alistair remarked remembering what some of his friends who had daughters had told him." But that doesn't mean a thing." He then retorted impatiently, "Our G.I. was killed in March! Did you ask him about the money?"
"Of course. He told us that he had never had much money and in fact, he'd got a big overdraft at his bank!'
"Have you checked?"
"No, Alistair, there was no reason to disbelieve him. We are sure that he wasn't involved."

Alistair felt frustrated being sure that he could have found out more if he had still been in charge. As it was he could do nothing.

What nobody had seen soon after the police had left, was Charlie Mackenzie locking the door of the shop, collapsing into his chair and pouring himself a large glass of Scotch. He could not believe how he had managed to lie or not to have been questioned further by the police. He went though all the things that had happened at the time. There was the murder of the American at the back of his shop by Andy's accomplice who was later shot by the Military Police. And then there were the lies he had told to the young sailor and his girl when he told them that the diamonds were false. His conscience was still troubling him about that, but he had given them £500 each to keep quiet about the murder. The police had failed to check the amount of his huge overdraft at his bank, which he had used to purchase the diamonds. It would have been difficult to explain why he needed that amount of money if they had.
Charlie's main worry now, was how to dispose of the diamonds that were lying in a security box at his bank. The proceeds would easily be enough to pay off his overdraft with a tidy sum left over. He had friends in Glasgow who would tell him how to dispose of them and now the war was over, they would again be able to make contact with jewellers in Amsterdam and Antwerp. He was confident that in a month or two he would be in the clear. After he had taken them from the young couple, he was not able to ask anybody where the diamonds had come from because of what happened so tragically and quickly. Although he suspected that they had been dishonestly obtained he convinced himself that he had bought them in good faith albeit at a low price compared to what they were really worth. When eventually he came to sell them he would make quite a handsome profit. Then, together with the sale of his stock, he would sell the shop and retire. It had not been a bad war after all he thought as he poured himself another large scotch.

Alistair was still troubled after Robert had left. He was sure that if they had really checked everything as he would have done a lot more could have been discovered. Someone must have known something about that diamond and Charlie Mackenzie's bank account would have been a good starting point to find out if that was where all that money came from. The money must have originated in Scotland as it was mainly in Scottish Bank notes. If only he had not retired he would have loved to get his teeth into that one. It seemed as though the present police had given up investigating anything further.
Alistair sat in his chair contemplating all this after Robert had left holding his tummy as his ulcer began to play up again. His bouts of indigestion had not troubled him since he retired but now because he wasn't there to be in control, things weren't being done properly and it began to worry him. He also wondered if he had missed something important during his own inquiries at Paisley. He was unable to get the thoughts of his last two unsolved cases out of his mind. There were far too many loose ends.
The pain seemed to increase and he felt a tightening in his chest and cursed what he thought was the start of the recurrence of his tummy troubles. He closed his eyes for a minute or two then went off to sleep.

An hour later Judy brought him a cup of tea but she could not wake him. She put the teacup gently down on the table by his side and held his hand. She could feel no pulse and, with tears filling her eyes, she went to the telephone to call the hospital for an ambulance.

Alistair's funeral was attended by a large contingent of police from both Glasgow and Paisley. Sergeants Robert Baillie and George Craythorn were two of the coffin bearers and he was taken to Paisley to be buried in the same cemetery where most of those small children were resting after that awful tragedy in December 1930.
"I think he would have liked that," Judy remarked..